S0-BRB-242

Murder
Most Fouled Up

MURDER MOST FOULED UP
DEAD BY THE LIGHT OF THE MOON
WHAT SHOULD YOU KNOW OF DYING?
A MATTER OF LOVE AND DEATH

Murder
Most Fouled Up

Tobias Wells

PUBLISHED FOR THE CRIME CLUB BY
DOUBLEDAY & COMPANY, INC.
GARDEN CITY, NEW YORK
1968

Library of Congress Catalog Card Number 68–18071
Copyright © 1968 by Doubleday & Company, Inc.
All Rights Reserved
Printed in the United States of America
First Edition

To my friend Cleo, who is, in a way,
responsible for these adventures

Murder
Most Fouled Up

1

Well, I was thirty years old and I'd been promoted to detective second grade and now what?

Beginning the morning of my thirtieth birthday (or maybe before that), I'd had this vague discomfort. It wasn't physical, not so far as I could tell, and Doc Albert had assured me at the time of my last checkup that I was in great shape for the shape I was in, but that wonderful old feeling that all was right with my world had evaporated. And in its place, this other thing, this "why doesn't something happen and if it does what could it be" feeling.

My mother said, and said curtly which was not at all like my mother, that I should grow up all the way. My father said, "Leave the boy alone, Helen. Let him live his own life." Which was unusual for my father, too, because he spoke sharply and I was hard put to remember

9

them having a disagreement, at least in my presence. I knew what she meant, of course, that I should get married, but I guess she was tired of saying it. God knows I was tired of hearing it, so that made us even. I would be married, damn it, but I hadn't been able to find anybody I wanted to marry so I just flat stopped looking. Fun and games, that was my motto, but even that took a bit of doing because my little black book was getting thinner and thinner. Susie Darren was Susie Henderson now and lived in New York. Candy Hecht had graduated from BU and had gotten herself engaged to a graduate student with a tall I.Q. and a short temper. Lorraine Allen had gone to Spain on a grant to paint. That left Gail Gregg, girl meter maid, and she bored me stiff half the time. So where was I? Out in left field.

"Way out in left field." I said it aloud involuntarily and Benedict, detective first grade and partner to detective second grade Knute Severson, looked up from his desk and asked, "What did you say, Knute?"

"I was just muttering in my beard," I told him. I shuffled some papers in front of me. "What did Granger say about these housebreaks? Do they tie in with any action in the other divisions? Two big ones in two days, smooth as a whistle. It's got to be a single operation."

"Captain Granger agrees. The Robbery Squad's correlating the information." Benedict checked his wristwatch and I realized he'd been looking at that wristwatch quite often since lunch.

"Another couple of hours," I said stretching. We'd gone on days twenty-four hours before and it took time to get used to the different routine. Usually I looked forward to the day shift, but of late it had been on the dull side. Crime takes a holiday in September. School's in and that kind of jazz. The long, hot summer is over.

Benedict nodded at my remark and lit a cigarette. I watched him with halfhearted interest. It had been, by and large, a very quiet day. Plenty of time to get caught up on reports. Writing reports made me more tired than anything else I could think of. It was hot and humid, too, summer or no summer. Too hot for September. I yawned and camouflaged it with my hand.

Benedict got up suddenly and walked to the water cooler. He walked quick-step which was not his normal way of walking. I put that together with the clock-watching bit and asked him when he came back, "Something special on the fire?"

His eyes were enigmatic behind his glasses. "What makes you think that?"

I blinked and sat up straighter. "Look, I'm not trying to be nosy. I was just making conversation . . ."

"I'm sorry, Knute. I'm edgy. You're right. There is something . . . but I'd rather not talk about it until it's more of a *fait accompli.*"

"Sure." I went back to shuffling papers, stacking them neatly. Benedict and I had been together almost two years now and we'd learned to get along together pretty good. He'd never pulled the clam act on me after we got to know each other so I didn't expect the cold shoulder, but his business was his business. He couldn't hurt my feelings.

"Knute . . ." he glanced around Division Two's detective room. Pinkerton and Dracutt were off in a corner

11

with Davoren, Captain Granger's clerk. It looked as though they were telling stories because just at that moment they threw their heads back in unison and laughed. "The thing is, Knute—" Benedict leaned confidentially across his desk,"—you know how Barbara has always wanted a child only they wouldn't let us adopt one because she's in a wheelchair? Well, we think we've found a way." He leaned back and looked at me expectantly, tried to suppress a grin of triumph.

"Gee, Benedict, that's great!" I lowered my voice. "What'd you do? Go out of state?"

He raised his eyebrows dramatically. "Out of country."

"Hey, that's terrific. From where, England, Scandinavia . . . ?"

"From Korea."

"From Korea!"

He leaned forward again. "Somebody's supposed to come tell us tonight if it's all set. It took some doing, pretty complicated, had to make arrangements to get her into this country and all that . . ."

"Her? It's a girl then."

"Kim. That's her name, Kim. She's six months old." He found it hard not to beam like a proud father.

I put out my hand. "Do you need a godfather?"

I'd never seen him look so happy. He shook my hand. "You're it." He composed himself. "That's if, of course, it works out."

"Sure it will."

"I hope so," breathed the man I used to think of as ice-cold Benedict. Then, like a couple of self-conscious kids, we turned away from each other and took up our paper

12

work. I couldn't help thinking, though, in that moment how much I envied Benedict. His wife, Barbara, was a wonderful gal, wheelchair or no wheelchair, and now they were going to be a family and raise a little kid. . . .

My outside phone rang. I reached for it, put it up to my ear. "Division Two," I identified myself, "Detective Severson."

"Oh, this is terrible, simply terrible. You must come right away. We came back from our trip and found her like this . . . oh, do come right away!"

I grabbed a pencil with my other hand. "Who is this? Where do you live? Slow down, will you?"

The female voice that had been wailing into my ear was jabbering to somebody else and then a man's voice came on, deep and sure. "Our name is Prescott," he said. "We live at 193 Marlborough Street. Please come at once. There's been a robbery and our daughter-in-law has been killed."

The Marlborough Street house looked pretty much like its neighbors on the outside, substantial and rather elderly. Inside it looked at first glance like a schizophrenic art museum torn between the classic traditional and avant-garde. Benedict and I, identifying ourselves to the big, gray-haired man who answered the door, exchanged glances.

"I'm Draper Prescott," the big man said when we'd made ourselves known. "Come this way." He might have been conducting a guided tour from the tone of his voice and Benedict and I, exchanging another glance, followed him. I couldn't help wondering if the pictures on the wall were all real; some of them, the kookier ones, obviously were, and if they were how come the burglar, if there had been a burglar, hadn't been interested? Not a one was out of line. Nobody had laid a finger on them, not even to clean them. I could see dust along the bottom of the frames. So maybe he didn't dig modern paintings but people paid big money for stuff like that.

We turned right into a small sitting room, handsomely furnished and empty of people, and followed Draper Prescott through a second door into a huge living room that must have run full-length along the side of the house. Long French doors with matching windows looked out from three directions on a weedy garden.

There was a woman standing at the far end of the room staring out through the doors she faced. Dust covers were still on the furniture, but one had been removed from a sofa and now covered something, someone on the floor. The woman standing at the far end turned as she heard us come in, moaned something and covered her mouth with a crumpled handkerchief. Her hair was fair and her figure slender, that's all I could tell from where I stood and then Benedict and I knelt down and lifted the dust cover.

When we stood up, the woman was still watching us with frantic eyes from the far French doors and Draper Prescott was making like a statue in front of the fireplace. "This is Mrs. Prescott," he said perfunctorily.

We nodded. "When the doorbell rings, it will be our men," Benedict informed them. "Would you prefer to tell us about this in another room?"

Mrs. Prescott spoke for the first time. Her voice was

high-pitched, ragged. "Couldn't we go outside . . . I need some air!"

She turned and grabbed at the handle of the French door like a drunk going to be sick. I started to follow her, heard Draper Prescott say matter-of-factly, "This, I believe, is the thing she was killed with."

He was indicating something on the floor near him and we walked around the undressed sofa to look. It was a crystal ashtray, pale lavender in color, chunky and heavy-looking. One side of it was smeared with what looked to be, but wasn't, strawberry jam.

"Don't touch it," cautioned Benedict.

"Of course not." Draper Prescott, duty done, marched off to join his wife. We went along after them.

Mrs. Prescott was seated, eyes closed, face pale, on a lacy white wrought-iron bench under a tree at the edge of a brick patio. The tree had peat moss around its base, but a few weeds were growing up through it. Prescott, standing sternly at the end of the bench, was removing a cigarette from a shiny case. Neither of them spoke.

"You say she was your daughter-in-law?" Benedict had his notebook out and I divided my concentration between what they were saying and listening for the arrival of Doc Albert and the rest of the boys.

"Yes. Her name was Dorinda Crewe Prescott." He lit the cigarette, disposed of lighter and case. "Mrs. Draper Shaw Prescott, II."

"What was she doing here? You said you'd been away —on a trip? Was she staying here?"

"No, she didn't stay here. We'd gone to Europe for three months." Prescott's tone was clipped much closer than the grass. Mrs. Prescott let out a sound that was between a sob and a sigh. "Dorinda had insisted on keeping an eye on the house, watering the plants, that sort of thing. She must have come here for that purpose."

"Where does she live?"

"In Wellesley Hills." He recited an address.

"And where is her husband, your son?"

"Shaw travels a great deal in his business. I called his office when we found her. His secretary said he is in St. Thomas looking into an investment there. Shaw is in mutual funds but he dabbles in real estate as well."

"Well, did you get in touch with him?" I blurted out.

Prescott turned cool gray eyes on me. "We have placed a long distance call and we have sent a cable. He was out when we called and we left a message."

"You said there had been a robbery," Benedict picked up the pace. "What was stolen? What makes you think the house was broken into?"

"Olivia, my wife, left her jewelry at home in the safe. I don't consider it wise to travel with expensive jewelry and she has a goodly amount of such trinkets so we've made it a practice to leave them behind. The safe has been opened and the jewelry is gone. It seemed rather academic to assume that the house had been broken into."

I bit my lip to keep from asking sarcastically, "Which came first, the chicken or the egg?" and Benedict did it for me but better.

"Which did you discover first, the theft or your daughter-in-law's body?"

16

"Dorinda. When we found her like that there was only one conclusion. I went to look at the safe."

"Which is where?"

"In our bedroom."

"It's all your fault," whined Mrs. Prescott suddenly. I'd almost forgotten she was there. "If you hadn't insisted that I not take my jewelry, Dorie would still be alive."

"Olivia," Prescott's tone was implacable and icily patient, "control yourself. Your reasoning lacks logic."

She looked at him. I was watching her eyes and they were completely hate-filled. Then she felt me watching and the expression went away. The handkerchief covered her eyes once more and she made weepy noises.

Something far off twanged. "I hear the doorbell," I told Benedict. "I'll let them in." I passed a coral-colored rosebush full of roses on the way in. It smelled like cinnamon. The last roses of summer were fading away.

Blasdell and Timmons with their fingerprint gear, Cowan with his camera and Doc Albert, bald head glistening, came in and went to work. I pointed out the ashtray to Blasdell and Timmons, watched a minute while the Doc examined the body. She'd been young, I judged somewhere in her twenties. Her hair was dark and straight, pulled back and held with a rubber band. It was the rubber band that wasn't stylish, I thought, because most of the girls her age and younger were wearing their hair plain but hanging loose over the back and shoulders. The older women still stuck to their bouffant poufs. Mrs. Prescott's hair was done that way, and I thought further that some teasing of the hair might have provided a cushion that could have protected Dorinda's long, thin head a little better. But more than likely not. That ashtray looked lethal.

Her body was thin, too, dressed in light colored jeans, a man-styled shirt and a cardigan sweater. If she'd come from Wellesley Hills dressed casually like that, she must have driven. I went back out into the garden to ask about her car. Maybe the thief had been greedy enough to take it. A car is a tangible thing, can be positively identified, sooner or later could be traced. When I got close enough for them to hear me, I asked, "Where's her car?"

Mrs. Prescott, who seemed to have composed herself, answered. "It's out by the garage. A red Volkswagen convertible. We saw it when we drove up, so we knew she was here." She crumbled again. "Poor Dorie. Shaw will be so upset."

"That's the list of the jewelry, then?" said Benedict looking up from his notebook.

"I think so," quavered Mrs. Prescott.

"We have an insurance policy that lists it in detail." Prescott's tone seemed to get dryer and dryer. "Unless, of course, the thief took that, too. It was in the safe."

"Let's go look at that safe," suggested Benedict. He closed his notebook and put it in his pocket.

"Oh, I couldn't go back in there . . ." Mrs. Prescott brought the handkerchief to her mouth once more. "With her lying in there . . ."

"I'll show you." Prescott walked away from us without a backward glance. I let Benedict go with him. Mrs.

Prescott might be more talkative without her husband around.

"Nice garden," I said conversationally. I tried to guess her age, put it somewhere in the sixties but she looked younger with her pale hair done all fancy and her slim figure.

"Oh. Yes. Well it was. But it's been neglected this summer. It's so difficult to get yardmen, truly reliable ones. Draper says he'd rather let it go to rack and ruin than to pay exorbitant sums of money to people who don't do anything. He says they let it go until just before you're due back, then they come in and get it all spruced up. That's when Dorie said she'd come and . . ." Her eyes, blue they were, a sort of faded blue, filled again.

"How often did she come, do you know?"

Mrs. Prescott shook her ash blond head. "She said something about once a week and I said that wasn't necessary but Prescott said let her do it, it would give her something to do, not having any children and all. . . ." Her mouth turned down as though a puppeteer had pulled on strings. "I just don't know how I can face Shaw and tell him . . . and tell him . . ."

I made a mental note to check on whether there was any fixed pattern as to when Dorinda Prescott made her visits. Neighbors here, friends in Wellesley Hills, somebody should know. I wanted to find out more about the girl anyway. It wasn't out of the realm of possibility that she'd told someone about her mother-in-law's baubles, had even given him access to the house.

"Do you know how they got in?"

"The thief?" She looked around at the windows of the

house as though they'd give her a clue. "No. I suppose they broke a window or jimmied—isn't that the right word?—a door. Draper talked once about getting a burglar alarm, but when he priced them he thought they were too expensive." She put her attention back on me. "I thought the police were supposed to determine things like how burglars get in." There was a certain amount of annoyance in her voice.

"We will," I promised her. I was recalling the rash of housebreaks of late. Entrance had been gained in a variety of ways, whatever seemed easier to the burglar, apparently, but there was a sameness to the methods of approach that was pretty cute. In every case, neighbors reported when questioned, they'd heard somebody banging after dark on the victim's front door, banging loudly and calling the householder's name. Sometimes these neighbors glanced out, saw the figure of a man, watched a minute, saw him go around the house and repeat the procedure at the back door. And again, in every instance, said neighbor thinking some friend had come to call, concluded that the Smiths or the Joneses or whoever they might be were not at home and their caller would find that out soon enough. With that conclusion, the neighbor returned to the television or what have you, heard no more from next door, and promptly forgot the whole incident. Meanwhile, the thief, sure that no one would bother him from within or without, went about his business unseen in the darkness.

I glanced back at the house and could see Blasdell checking the French doors and Timmons working at the windows. They'd make the rounds till they found it.

Where there was a hole, there was a potential entrance. Door or window, jalousie or screen, it was much the same as what goes up must come down. Whatever could be closed could be opened, whatever could be locked could be unlocked.

"I don't understand how they got into the safe," Mrs. Prescott said suddenly. "I'm quite sure I closed it."

I looked at her. "Maybe you didn't."

"Oh, but I know I did." She shook her head wisely. "Yes. I remember. I closed it tight. I wonder how they got into it."

I eyed her warily. "Did your daughter-in-law know the combination?"

"Dorie?" Her expression was startled. "Of course not. Whyever would Draper tell her the combination of his safe?"

"You mean you don't know it?"

Her eyelids drooped. "No. I don't have a good memory for things like numbers. And Draper didn't want it written down somewhere where someone could find it."

I frowned. It sounded reasonable but at the same time it sounded unreasonable. What if he were away and needed something in the safe, or what if something happened to him, then what? I started to ask her but just then Benedict and Prescott came out the French doors with a sheaf of papers, so I didn't. Another time. Doc Albert was coming out, too. It looked as though the preliminaries to the main event were over.

2

I volunteered to make an off-duty run out to Wellesley and see what I could find out about Dorinda Prescott. I knew Captain Granger was surprised, Benedict, too, but neither of them showed it. Granger only said, "See what the chief of police has to say, if anything," and I told him I'd check in at the station as a matter of courtesy.

Benedict, the boy-most-likely-to-work-overtime, was this night eager to get going. He hurried through the details of the Prescott burglary. No fingerprints other than the dead woman's and some latent daubs of Mr. and Mrs. Prescott, Sr., who, surprisingly enough, made very little fuss about having their fingers inked. Come to think of it, public cooperation with the police was becoming a source of amazement to me. I guessed I was getting cynical and the thought disturbed me. Lots of the guys did, I knew that, but I'd never expected to grow calloused. Now I could add that to my little list of worries.

"Knute went to the neighbors'," Benedict told Granger and looked expectantly at me.

"They tinkled the glass at a kitchen window," I took up the tale. "Nice neat job, undoubtedly quickly and quietly done. No fingerprints, of course. Gained entrance that way and then we figure they went straight upstairs because nothing was disturbed downstairs. Except the ashtray. They knew where they were going and why, that's pretty clear."

"Seems obvious the ashtray's the murder weapon." Granger sat back, pyramided his fingertips, a customary gesture. "How do you figure it? The girl walked in on them?"

"Something like that. The key to the front door was on a ring in her jeans pocket. The killer must have heard her, come down the stairs quietly, picked up the first heavy thing at hand and whammo, let her have it."

"Which indicates he didn't carry a gun."

"Maybe. But guns make noise. Crystal ashtrays don't. If she came at night, she must have turned some lights on but he, in turn, must have switched them off because they weren't burning when the Prescotts arrived home the next morning."

Benedict, listening to this exchange, looked at his watch.

"You go ahead, Benedict," I said. "I'll fill the captain in the rest of the way."

"It's something urgent," Benedict said apologetically.

"Get out of here, then," Granger scowled at him without animosity. "You're overtime already."

24

Benedict smiled gratefully. "Thanks, Captain. See you in the morning, Knute."

"I've asked somebody from the Robbery Squad to come in first thing," Granger said in parting. "Then we'll see where we stand in this picture."

When the door had closed behind Benedict, I referred to my notebook. "Number 195, occupants, two maiden ladies, the Misses Ada and Estelle Vancouver. They heard someone at the Prescott's door at about 8:00 P.M. or so. It was a man, according to them, and he was calling, 'Mr. Prescott! Hi, Mr. Prescott!' They debated whether they should go out and tell him the Prescotts were in Europe, decided to mind their own business. In Miss Ada Vancouver's words, 'Nobody thanks a nosy old-maid neighbor.'"

Granger grunted. I knew what he was thinking. So-called nosy neighbors were dying out and that made police work all the harder.

"Number 197, occupants Mr. and Mrs. Henry Stone. Mrs. Stone is in the hospital for a gall bladder operation and Mr. Stone was visiting her last night. He didn't get home until after ten and, according to him, the Prescott house was as dark as a tomb."

"Not a very good choice of words."

"He didn't think so either. He turned red as a beet when he realized what he'd said. Now, let's backtrack. I'm giving this to you in pieces beginning with the first known contact by the burglar. As I said, Dorinda Prescott could have turned on some lights when she came in, but the Misses Vancouver didn't see any, they'd gone to the other side of the house to watch television. The only people who thought they saw a light were the Canfields directly across the street. Mrs. Canfield is hard of hearing and Mr. Canfield is losing his sight so they're not the most reliable of witnesses. It was Mrs. Canfield who thought she saw lights sometime around 9:00 P.M. and Mr. Canfield, after she'd remarked on the lights, said she was mistaken. She wasn't too sure either because when she looked again the place was dark. Either she saw a reflection, or she looked over just before the killer doused the electricity. We'll know more about that when the Doc gives us the time of death."

"How about the people beyond the adjacent houses? In back of the Prescott place?"

I shook my head. "Nothing. The Prescotts have a garden, overgrown at that, with trees and bushes that pretty well hide the house from the rear. One party beyond the Misses Vancouver was away, the ones on the other side of the Stones were throwing a cocktail orgy and they wouldn't have noticed anything in all the confusion."

"Surely one of them knew the victim, knew that she came there."

"The Vancouver ladies did but they didn't know when and how often. They only knew that when they saw the little red car, it was the Prescott's daughter-in-law, and I quote."

"Doesn't sound like a very neighborly neighborhood." Granger pushed back his chair, got up and stretched.

"Typical. Maybe I'll do better in Wellesley. I'm extremely interested in Dorinda Crewe Prescott and her husband."

"You mean because of the safe. Somebody had to have the combination."

"If they didn't, we've got an expert safecracker to deal with and most of the old-timers are dead, jailed, or even retired. Nobody takes the time to learn the trade anymore, they tell me. They'd rather blow it quick with plastics." I stood up and jingled my car keys.

"How high was the score?"

"According to the insurance, seventy-eight thousand. Mostly diamond rings and bracelets. One fancy-sounding necklace."

"Matthew, Mark, Luke, and John. And they tell me that crime doesn't pay."

"Yeah. That's what they say. Benedict has the list in his report and we'll get a bulletin out to the pawnshops in the morning, not that I expect it to turn up there. Meanwhile, I'll get going to the hinterlands and I'll let you know what I find out in the A.M."

I took the new toll road to Wellesley, clear sailing. The brick police station sat nicely in the middle of a big grass plot with apartments for the aged behind it. A good arrangement, in case any of the old folks needed help day or night.

The chief was off duty but his deskman called him up and he gave him the okay to fill me in on anything they knew about Dorinda Prescott, which turned out to be next to nothing.

"She's been active in a peace petition they've been circulating in town," the sergeant told me. "She came in here one day to see if it was okay if they rang doorbells and I referred her to the Selectmen's Office. That's all I know about the lady."

"How about the husband?"

"An old traffic violation five years back. That's all."

The trouble with people who don't get into trouble is that they're virtually anonymous. "I want to take a look-see at her house," I told the sergeant, "how about some company from the Wellesley police?"

He looked doubtful. "We're pretty short-handed. Couple of guys on late vacations, plays hell with the schedules. You got a search warrant?"

"Right here."

"Well . . . maybe Dennehy can meet you over there." He talked into the radio, which eventually squawked back at him. "He'll get there before you do," said the sergeant when he got back to me. "He's in the Cliff estates now."

I almost got lost following his directions but it wasn't his fault, the roads were winding. When I pulled up in front of the big white house, a pale blue Wellesley car was waiting for me, its red light flashing.

"I'm Severson," I said to the officer who got out of it.

"I'm Dennehy." We shook hands.

I used a key from the dead girl's key ring to open the door and fumbled along the wall for lights. The carpet was green and wall-to-wall, the walls were a paler tone of the same color. Everything in the house looked new and unused. It was nicely decorated but sterile. I wondered what the poor thin young woman with the traveling husband did with her days before she ran out of them.

The only answers I got to this question were on a shiny

walnut desk, a stack of papers filled with signatures, the peace petition; and a photograph of a handsome guy looking solemn and somehow theatrical in a silver frame.

Officer Dennehy, a big pink-complexioned guy with innocent eyes, frowned at the picture. "I've seen him somewhere before."

"I guess that's the husband. Draper Shaw Prescott, II. Called Shaw."

Dennehy shook his head. "The name doesn't mean anything. It's the face that's familiar."

"I'm going to hit up the neighbors. Want to come with me?"

"Yeah. I'd like to." He looked concerned. "Maybe I'd better call in first."

We went back through the house, shutting off lights as we went. I carried the petition and the picture with me. While I stashed them in my car, Dennehy made radio contact with the sergeant. When I came back to him, he was beaming.

"It's all right. Things are quiet." The smile faded. "Things are always quiet except when the teen-agers get ants in their pants."

"Don't knock it." But I knew what he meant.

He followed right on my heels to the house next door. We should have driven, the yards were big enough for a scout hike. We walked up a curved driveway and pushed the nose of a brass lion's head that was doubling for a doorbell. After a few minutes, a dainty little miss in a short purple dress opened the door.

I told her who we were and her eyes lit up. "Oh, I'll

bet it's about Mrs. Prescott. Come in, I'll get my mother and father."

Father and mother, Hinchliffe, their name was, looked like magazine ads. "We were just on our way out." Mrs. Hinchliffe looked up at me through thick lashes.

"I'm sorry to delay you. . . ."

"God, man," said Hinchliffe, "that's all right. What's this world coming to if we can't devote a few minutes to a departed friend?"

The daughter of the house, eyes wide and glistening, followed us all into the living room. Where the house next door had been a symphony in greens, this one was a rhapsody in shades of blue.

"Do sit down, Detective Severson," Mrs. Hinchliffe dimpled at me, and arranged herself on a light blue velvet tufted bench.

"Yes, indeed. You, too, Officer. Either of you gentlemen care for a drink?"

"No, thanks." Dennehy and I answered Hinchliffe in unison. I thought our host looked slightly disappointed as he took a seat beside his wife. Almost absentmindedly he said, "Linda, this isn't for you. Go on into the den and watch TV."

Miss High School stuck her tongue out at him behind his back and flounced out. I was pretty certain she was listening from behind the door. But then, I reminded myself, I was getting cynical.

"You haven't caught the man yet?" asked Mrs. Hinchliffe. She spoke as though she naturally assumed we had run right out and picked him up.

"Come now, Evelyn." Hinchliffe gave me a man-to-man grin. His teeth were positively pearly. "What do you think they are, miracle men? They just found the body this afternoon. Isn't that right?"

"Right," I said. Dennehy leaned forward, elbow on the arm of the chair he sat in, chin on his hand. Perfect picture of sophomore at seminar.

"I wondered when she didn't come home last night." Evelyn Hinchliffe batted her eyelashes. As eyelashes go, they went further than most. I wondered if they were real, decided not. "We often have coffee together in the morning. I went over early, but no Dorinda. That's how I knew she hadn't been home. Well, I didn't *know*, but I thought about it." She raised her hands in a pretty gesture, dimpled again. "I told my husband she'd spent the night on the town."

"Was she in the habit of staying out all night then?"

Mr. and Mrs. Hinchliffe exchanged a merry look. "Dorinda?" trilled Evelyn. "Heavens, no! That's what made it so amusing. It's a family joke. Between ourselves, Greg and I have always called her Dorinda-the-daring darling. Because she wasn't. You see?"

"She wasn't a darling?"

"No, silly. She wasn't daring. Not at all. Her name should have been Prim-and-proper Priscilla." She giggled. "That's another family joke." They twinkled at each other like the young marrieds in the movies.

"How often did she go to her in-laws' house? Did she have a regular schedule?"

Evelyn Hinchliffe gave the question her personal consideration. "Yes, I guess you could say she went on a regular basis. She didn't know much about house plants so she

31

asked me, right after they'd gone away, how often she should water them. I said it depended, but that every three or four days should be about right. She went in every three or four days, just as I said. Dorinda was like that. If someone said, in passing, that a person should take vitamins, she'd take vitamins. If you recommended olive oil for fingernails, she'd soak her nails in olive oil. She was like a well-brought-up little girl, did as she was told."

Every three or four days. If the house had been staked out before the robbery, would the burglars have picked that up? Obviously not, or they wouldn't have gone in when they did. They would have set a date for the day after if they knew the pattern. That would give them two or three days' leeway.

"Did she have any family? Do they live around here?" What was her background, I wanted to know. Was she to the manor born or had she found herself a bed of roses? If it was the latter, she could have been ripe for playing accomplice even though I didn't feel that she had been. The accidental intrusion fitted better. So far.

"Her mother is dead," Evelyn told me. I thought the Hinchliffes were getting a bit restless now. "Her father is in Washington. Something to do with the Treasury, I believe."

"State Department," amended her husband. He sneaked a look at his watch.

I got the hint and stood up. "One last question—you intimate that she wouldn't have been interested in another man. Would she have been interested in money for any reason?"

They rose together, looked wide-eyed together. "Dorinda?" Evelyn Hinchliffe gave me a smile I entitled condescending. "She was a Crewe, you know. *The* Crewes."

"Hell," said Greg, "to put it bluntly, they are loaded." He grinned at me. We were brothers in life, we believed in calling a spade a spade, his smile told me.

"Thanks for the time." I made my adieus and headed for the door with Dennehy right behind me.

"You're welcome," replied Greg. "Any time we can be of help. . . ." I glimpsed Linda's purple miniskirt disappearing at the far end of the hall but nobody else caught it. Graciously dismissed by *mère* and *père,* we began our hike across the carved velvet lawn, at least that's what it looked like under the quaint gas lamps that illuminated the landscape.

Something moved, came out of the bushes. It was Linda Hinchliffe, eyes shining in the dark, arms hugging herself in the cool night air. "I can help you," she said. She bubbled somewhat like her mother. This was a great and grand new game. "But I didn't want them to hear. They think I'm an infant or something."

"What's on your mind?" I asked her, stopping short. Dennehy nearly bumped into me, so close was he behind.

"It's Mr. Prescott. Shaw. Her husband." She looked around in perfect spy fashion. "I think he goes for other women."

"What makes you think that?"

She tossed her hair airily. "Just the way he acted, you know. The way he'd look at a girl. He's very handsome and she isn't—wasn't very pretty."

"Anybody in particular that he looked at?"

33

"Not really." Her eyelids dropped. She had long lashes, too. Maybe mother's weren't phony. She made a gesture with her hands, an echo of her mother's mannerisms. Was it some Indian poet who had likened hands to pale moths? Or was that pale hands I love beside the Shalimar? "Just everybody." Up with the eyelids. "Even me." A soft giggle, half depreciation, half satisfaction. Then, "If I were you, I'd look into his whereabouts. I mean, seriously."

"We did, Miss Hinchliffe. He's in the Caribbean." I said thanks and we left her there thinking deep thoughts.

3

Dennehy's disciplined tongue loosened when we got back to the cars and he offered me several theories. I nodded and told him we were exploring those very avenues but I was looking beyond the Prescott house to its second neighbor, an ultramodern job perched on a hill to my right. I decided it wouldn't do any harm to pay another call as long as I was there and, out of courtesy, asked Dennehy if he wanted to ride over with me. The words were hardly out of my mouth before he started for my car, only to be halted in mid-movement by a squawk from his radio. He looked disappointed and went over to answer the call.

"I'm sorry," he said hanging up the radio phone. "There's a husband and wife hassle down on Barton Road. I guess I'll have to leave you."

"Thanks for the help. I'll see you around." I opened my car door.

"My pleasure," said Officer Dennehy as though he meant it. He started his motor and took off down the driveway, red light making circles. There was one lad who wasn't soured on his job, that was sure.

I read the name on the fancy mailbox at the foot of the next driveway. K. K. Mason. "All right, Mr. and/or Mrs. Mason," I said aloud as I drove in, "let's see what you have to say about your late neighbor."

There was a dog inside the house, a dog that yapped like a little dog, and finally I made out its shape through the modernistic glass panel beside the stark door. It looked like an animated mop, a Pekinese. You didn't see many Pekinese any more, I thought idly, and rang the lighted doorbell once more.

I heard footsteps, feminine footsteps in heels, and then somebody opened the door.

She was very blond, almost platinum, and very curvy. She was also no spring chicken. "Yes?" she asked in a kind of purr. The mop peeked around her ankles and made shrill, threatening noises.

I told her who I was, produced evidence. "Oh, Pujums, do be quiet," she told the dog, moving it out of the way with an adroit foot. "Come in, Detective Severson." The door opened wider. "I have to be so careful living all alone as I do. . . ."

She swayed as she led the way into the living room. Some of the sway was reminiscent of the late Marilyn Monroe in full flight and some of it suggested that the lady might have had a little drink-y. The Pekinese had

36

taken Dennehy's place at my heels, an unfair exchange no matter how you looked at it.

"Won't you sit down, Detective Severson?" She pointed out a creation for sitting known as a butterfly chair done up in orange canvas and I reluctantly lowered myself into it.

"I'm having a drink." She indicated a partially full glass on a free-form cocktail table. "I won't ask you to have one because I know the police don't drink while they're on duty."

I could have told her it was off duty, but it was better the way it was. She'd look pretty good from a distance, I decided, but up close there was a certain leatheriness to her skin. The striped knit dress she wore had been designed for a younger girl, although I didn't have any real quarrel with her wearing it. She had a good figure.

"I'm inquiring about Dorinda Prescott, Mrs. Mason." I didn't bother to ask if she was Miss or Missus, it kind of stood out all over her.

"Oh, yes." She reached for her drink. I thought her hand shook a little. "I heard it on the radio. Tragic."

The dog sniffed around my ankles, reminded me of an anteater.

"Did you know Mrs. Prescott well? Did she say anything about her in-laws' house, perhaps she'd seen someone hanging around?"

Mrs. Mason shook her bright head and raised her drink, managed to get mouth and glass connected. When she set it down, empty, she went on. "I knew her, of course. We were so-so friendly. But we moved in different circles. Except for big parties around the holidays, things

37

like that." Drinking or not, her eyes looked alert. "She had a husband, you see, and I don't. Divorcées seldom mix with ball-and-chainers." She smiled and I realized she must have been a beauty a few years back. She was no plain Jane now.

I nodded. It figured. Having seen both Dorinda and Mrs. Mason, I couldn't have expected them to have much in common. I'd put a couple more polite questions and leave her to her cocktail hour—or hours. I asked the routine one, did she know when Dorinda Prescott went in to her in-laws' house and only half-listened to her denial.

But then she said, "Are you going after him?" I thought her eyes glittered.

"If you mean Prescott, he wasn't even in the country when it happened."

She raised here eyebrows. "Too bad. He would have been the logical suspect." She got up, walked over to a bar built into the wall, and began to mix another drink. I hadn't given Shaw Prescott too much thought before I'd come out to Wellesley, but now he was beginning to intrigue me.

"Why do you say that?"

She turned, looking wise. "Isn't it always the husband? Especially one who clearly believes he is God's gift to femininity?"

"Did he play around?" I asked bluntly.

She turned away and stirred her fresh drink, came back then to where I could see her face better.

"Don't they all?" Her face was a mask so it didn't matter whether I saw it or not. "But if you're asking

38

for names and numbers, I can't give you any. All I know is, she wasn't in his category. Not one bit."

"But they had similar backgrounds. At least, I understood that she had money, too."

"You misunderstood me. I said she wasn't in his category. I didn't say she wasn't in his league. She came from a wealthy family, all right, had impeccable manners, went to all the right schools, I know that much about her. But she was a zero. She'd buy a designer dress and it would look like a bargain basement model on her. She'd go into some fancy hairdresser in Boston every so often and by the time she got home, the careful coiffure became a nothing. She always fell back into place, no matter how she was arranged. A tissue tracing of a girl that you couldn't make third dimensional, no matter how much you tried."

Kay-Kay Mason, all of a sudden, interested me. I said, "You haven't got a beer in your ice chest, have you?"

The eyebrows rose again but the face stayed in place. "Why not?" I watched her leave the room, return with a bottle of Heinekins. "German. Okay?"

"Fine." She opened it at the bar, brought it over with a glass. Because she'd made no comment, I told her I was off duty. I didn't want her to lose her illusions about cops taking a brew.

I watched while she poured the beer, she was a woman to watch, then urged, "Tell me about them. Anything you can think of. I saw her after she was dead and I haven't seen him at all."

Mrs. Mason went back to her chair, one that stood on a single white pedestal, and tasted her drink. "I like to talk about people," she said frankly. "It's satisfying to play the cat occasionally. But, when somebody's dead . . ." She picked up the glass again. "It's not so much fun after that."

"Don't think of it as idle gossip. Right now it looks as though Mrs. Prescott was the victim of a frightened burglar, but we can't take that for granted. You said her husband seemed like a logical suspect and there's some truth in that. There have been cases where the husband set up the burglary, hired an assassin. Could be that Shaw Prescott did have a hand in this thing. What can you tell me about them, about the way they were in each other's company? We may not win any wars but it might help with the strategy planning."

She looked thoughtful. "He was . . . I would say, tolerant. Almost could see him thinking, she's a poor thing but my wife, that sort of thing. Last New Year's Eve I threw a shindig, open house. Invite the neighbors, it's better than having them complain to the police that you're raising hell." She grinned at me. "They were here fairly early, I think they were going to a midnight supper at his parents' house. Anyway, they were among the first to arrive so I was still pretty sober." Another grin, man to man. No, more like woman to man, only a completely unaffected woman.

"She was wearing a sad little black velvet number. Black hasn't been in the last couple of seasons, you know, and it wasn't a good color on her anyway. Her skin was too sallow. But he looked like Mr. Esquire as usual. If I'd been a bit more under the influence, I might have asked him why he didn't take her in hand, tell her what to wear. I didn't, of course, and to tell you the truth, I didn't have to. I knew."

"You mean he wanted her to look like that?"

"Sure. The plain little hen shows up the brilliant cock. He would stay near her all evening, pay polite attention, and let people come to him. I was sort of out of line when I suggested he played around. That was the bitter-bite in Kay-Kay Mason talking then. I never saw him make a false move."

"Interesting," I said, and drank my beer.

"I met his parents once. A year ago Christmas, I think it was. The father is like ice and the mother is one of those women who's spent her life playing the feather-brained nitwit. Sure she is! Like Gracie Allen was. Dumb like a fox."

Now it was my turn to grin. When I'd sobered, I said, "You don't think there's a chance that Dorinda might have had a hand in the burglary, either on purpose or inadvertently?"

She shrugged. Her glass was empty again. "Inadvertently, I don't know. Deliberately, I'd say never in a million years."

"They lived in a good-sized house over there. Did they have servants?"

She laughed and headed for the bar. "You're living in a dream world. We're lucky to get a woman for the day out here. If they do come, you spend your time running them back and forth from the MBTA." She turned to look at me. "We do share a gardener. An old Italian guy from Wellesley's Back Bay. Named Tonio Gigglio."

She shook her head. "He wouldn't be mixed up in any-thing like that."

I wrote down the name and finished my beer. Note-book still out, I asked, "Do you know the names of any of their friends?"

"Sorry. I don't think they had too many. Their social life seemed to gravitate around mater and pater. And, of course, he traveled a lot." She'd mixed her drink by then, gin and Schweppes, it was, and added, "Want an-other beer?"

"No, thanks." I stood up, put the notebook away. "I've got to run along. Thanks for your help."

Pujums, whom I'd quite forgotten, came from behind a long, low sofa near the window wall and went into his dog-bite-man routine.

"Hush," Kay-Kay Mason told him, and interrupted his forward progress toward my ankles with that same adroit foot. The dog sat down and blinked up at her with hypo-thyroid eyes. "He's a pest," she said to me. "And what about that stupid name? My ex-husband named him and the mutt's not bright enough to change. But then, neither was my ex-husband. I'll see you to the door."

I let her go ahead of me, partly out of politeness and partly because she was so pleasant to watch. "Thanks again," I said as we parted.

"As my ex would be pleased to tell you, I like men. So, the pleasure was all mine." And all I could think as I drove away was that Kay-Kay Mason was wasting what looked to be a great talent. I wondered what her ex was doing on these fine fall nights. Probably, she was an alcoholic. More than likely. But, was this a before or after picture? A Pekinese named Pujums would drive almost anybody to the bottle.

I hoped to God I'd never be like that. Somewhere between forty and fifty with nothing to do but feel the miseries. I checked the clock on my dashboard. After ten. I'd better get home. I'd have another beer and let my cat, Mein Hair, out. No, I thought again as I turned onto the Mass. Turnpike Extension, I sure as hell never wanted to be like that.

4

When I got into the office the next morning, Benedict was poring over a sheaf of papers that looked like reports. He said, "Good morning. Robbery Squad sent these over." And I said, "Get your nose out of those things and tell me what happened last night. Are you going to be a father?"

He put the papers down on the desk and beamed. It was maybe the happiest smile I'd ever seen on Benedict's face. I asked, "When?"

"They've got somebody lined up to bring the baby over and they think it may be soon." No maybe about it, I'd never seen him look so pleased, so kind of young. "All the preliminaries are in the works. If everything meshes in time, all the red tape, they hope by next weekend." He snaked a long piece of paper out of his pocket.

"Barbara's given me a shopping list. Clothes and stuff. I'm going to start on it at lunch."

I punched him lightly on the shoulder. "Good show." Somebody called our names then and we looked up to see Davoren standing in the captain's doorway. "Bring in those reports," he called.

Benedict gathered them up and we went into Granger's office, greeting Casey and Cowan as we passed, who were seated at their desks in the corner. I waved to Dracutt across the room. He was on the phone and saluted back.

Granger had on a new suit and that shook me up a little. It was a Glen plaid, pretty snazzy, and I wondered what had lifted him out of his traditional dark blue rut. "Sit down," he said. "Have you had a chance to go over the burglary sheets?"

I shook my head. "I just got in."

"I glanced at them," Benedict laid the sheets on Granger's desk. "There are definite similarities."

"The business of calling out at the front and back doors," agreed Granger. "Look them over, Knute. You'll see what I mean. And these aren't the only ones, you know. Last month, a half dozen; the month before, ten here and in surrounding towns. These are just the most recent ones."

The Louisburg Square residence of Arthur Cloy, I read, had been burglarized four days before, on Friday night. Jewelry and cash had been stolen, approximate value not yet determined, but there had been two thousand dollars in cash which Cloy stated he'd drawn out of the bank to buy a new car. "I get a kick out of doling it out in cash," he'd commented when questioned. Neighbors had reported hearing someone at Cloy's door, had reacted much the same as the Prescotts' neighbors. Mr. and Mrs. Cloy had gone to the Red Sox game, then to a late supper, got home about 1:00 A.M. They didn't discover the theft until Saturday morning.

On Saturday night, the Charles Phelpses on Beacon Street had been hit for two fur coats, a diamond wristwatch, and four diamond rings of one, two, three, and four carats respectively. "Charles bought me a bigger one every fifth anniversary," according to Mrs. Phelps. One Richard Rotman, visiting nearby, was pulling into a parking space when he noticed two men pounding on the Phelpses' front door at about 8:00 P.M. He mentioned it to the friend he was visiting, but the friend was so eager to introduce Richard to a girl his wife had found for Rotman that he paid no attention. Richard Rotman couldn't really say what the men looked like. It was getting dark and he didn't look too closely. He was under the impression they were fairly young. "That is, not old," and dressed in ordinary clothes. The Phelpses, during this time, had been away at the Cape, closing their summer place.

In both burglaries, entrance had been gained through a window at the rear of the house and nothing had been taken other than personal items. Nothing else had been disturbed, it was as though the thieves knew exactly what they were looking for, went right to it, and took off. Not that it was especially hard to find; Mrs. Phelps kept her jewelry in a jewelry box on her dresser and her fur coats in her closet. The Cloys kept their valuables in a tin box on the top shelf of a linen closet. The burglars took box and all.

I looked up. Granger was talking baseball, asking Benedict whether he thought the Red Sox had a chance at the pennant. I didn't think Benedict knew anything about baseball, but he said, "With the Twins, Detroit, and Chicago in there battling, the team with the breaks will be the one to win. Minnesota's the most dependable team, I think, but the schedule favors Detroit. Still, I think we've got an excellent chance."

"If I can interrupt your sports analysis," I spoke lightly, "I'd like to ask a question. Do any of these people know one another, belong to the same clubs, anything like that?"

"Robbery is checking on that very thing. Sticks out like a sore thumb, doesn't it?" Granger straightened his necktie absentmindedly. It was a dark red club tie with little silver triangles sprinkled here and there. He certainly was dolled up. "They want you men to talk to the Prescotts again along those lines."

"There must be some connection." I thought out loud.

"What did you find out in Wellesley?" Granger wanted to know.

I gave them a terse rundown on the Hinchliffes and Kay-Kay Mason. "The most significant reaction was *cherchez l'homme*. Shaw Prescott comes across as a character right out of a Victorian novel. I think an interview with him will be interesting, as soon as we can get hold of him, that is. Have the Prescott Seniors had any word as to when he's coming back?"

"No word from them this morning," Granger reported. "If these burglaries are connected, and it sure looks as though they are, it pretty well rules out Shaw Prescott, doesn't it? I'm guessing you're considering that he might have hired somebody to do away with his wife. You don't mean to indicate that you believe he was playing games with the airlines, do you? Flying in and out of Puerto Rico, or wherever he was? That kind of business sounds good in murder mysteries but it's a whale of a lot simpler in theory than in fact."

"I know. One late flight and your little scheme is shot full of holes. We can check it out with the airlines, of course, but I have a strong hunch we'll find that young Mr. Prescott really was in St. Thomas as advertised. Still, I'm anxious to talk to him."

"I'll call the Prescotts and tell them we're coming over." Benedict got out of his chair, was halted by the ringing of the captain's phone.

"Granger," the captain identified himself and then listened. "You say he's there now? In that case, Detectives Benedict and Severson will come right over." He listened again. "We're doing our best, Mr. Prescott." He spoke after a longer pause, raising his eyebrows at us. "Yes, we've alerted the pawnshops and we're watching the known fences, using your insurance list for descriptions. I had a call from your insurance company early this morning. They're making their own investigation, said they began right after you notified them yesterday. And, since the crime was discovered only yesterday, I'd say we were making as much progress as could be expected at this early date, wouldn't you?"

He closed his eyes and listened some more. I could hear Prescott's voice rumbling in the telephone. Then,

"Yes, Mr. Prescott, you might say that murder does place your case high on the priority list. As I said before, Detectives Benedict and Severson will be right over to talk to your son."

There was more from Prescott that I couldn't make out and then the definite bang of a receiver. Granger looked pained, hung up his own phone. "Moses on the mountain," he swore. "Shaw Prescott flew in late last night. He'll see you now, but don't let that Prescott push you around. St. Francis of Assisi!" Draper Prescott got two swear phrases.

Shaw Prescott was waiting for us in the garden. An umbrella table had been set up and he was sitting at it, drinking coffee and wearing sunglasses. The remains of his breakfast were evident on a plate pushed to one side. When his father brought us out to him, brought us, I thought, the way you bring in a necessary evil, he waved vaguely at the plate and drawled, "Can't we get someone to take that away?"

To my surprise, Mr. Prescott picked up the dishes and went. "Sit down," invited Shaw Prescott. The September sun glittered on his silver-gold hair. He had on his Caribbean clothes, I gathered, a pair of white ducks so well washed and worn that they looked almost like velvet, a bright blue silky-looking sports shirt and a yellow ascot tucked in at the neck. On his feet were white espadrilles. Pretty, pretty, I thought further, and we sat down.

"I've just gotten up," he told us, removing his sunglasses and rubbing his eyes. His eyes were gray like his father's, but not so hard. They did look sleepy.

"I got the first flight I could get," he went on, "but

even so, it was early morning before I got to bed." He smiled at us, showing whiter-than-white teeth against the tan of his face, smiled only briefly, then let the smile fade out. "That's why I can't seem to grasp this business. My parents told me, but I can't believe it. You understand what I mean?" Now he looked several ways, solemn, hurt, bewildered. "Dorie." He all but whispered her name. "Tell me, please. The way you see it, without any frills. How did it happen?"

Benedict cleared his throat. "Sometime Sunday evening, we think around nine o'clock, your wife drove to this house and let herself in with her key. We can only assume that she came at that time to make sure everything was in order for your parents' return. Sometime prior to your wife's arrival, about eight or eight-thirty, neighbors heard someone at the door here and, again, we assume that this disturbance was caused deliberately by the burglars. It's a common enough subterfuge, but it seems to be a *modus operandi* for this crew.

"They subsequently gained entrance through a rear window after breaking the glass and were, still another assumption, in the house when Dorinda Prescott arrived. One of them, at least, heard your wife come in, sneaked downstairs, and struck her on the back of the head with a heavy crystal ashtray. That's the way it seems to have happened."

Shaw shut his eyes and shuddered. He put the sunglasses back on. "She was always doing good deeds," he mourned. "I used to chide her about it. Someday one of your underdogs is going to bite you, Dorie, I used to say."

51

He turned the blank stare of the glasses on us. "I didn't know how prophetic that was."

I frowned at him. "You're suggesting that she could have known the thieves? That she'd met them, working for some cause or another, and that she came here to talk them out of it, something like that?"

His tan brow wrinkled. "No—no. I didn't mean that. How could Dorie know anything about criminals? She didn't do social work, that sort of business. I only meant she was doing a good deed by keeping an eye on the house for my folks. It really wasn't necessary, but she insisted. If she hadn't been so conscientious. . . ." He turned away from us in dejection.

His father came out purposefully through the French doors, ready to do battle now that he'd rid himself of the plate, that was obvious. "Have they told you what they're doing, if anything, to catch the murderer of your wife?" he demanded.

"Not yet," said Benedict smoothly. "We were waiting for you."

Draper Prescott glared at him, then sat down. "Here I am. Tell me your fairy story."

"This burglary was one of three over the weekend and the evidence indicates that they were the work of one gang. This same gang has been busy all summer, here in Boston and in the suburbs. We've been looking for them for some time; not only have we been looking but the various police forces in the other areas affected have been looking and the Robbery Squad as well. All of us, and particularly the guys in Robbery, have contacts. We know the boys most likely to succeed at tailgating, robbery, breaking and entering, burglary, and larceny. They're all specialized today, like every other profession. But this is a new operation and none of our usual sources have come up with anything, so it's been a long, slow process. That's where we stand this morning, Mr. Prescott, and the chances are these men we're seeking will go underground deeper than ever now because they're not only wanted for burglary, which carries pretty high penalties, but for murder, too."

Draper Prescott looked disdainful. "What you're telling me is that you haven't found out anything and aren't likely to do so. No wonder insurance premiums are so expensive."

Benedict's expression was bland. "I am merely explaining procedures. Hundreds of men, in one way or another, are working on this case and were working on it even before it actually happened. Sooner or later, one of those skilled men will pull a string that will eventually unravel the puzzle. Then, if we're fortunate enough to collect the acceptable sort of evidence to go with our knowledge, you'll have the satisfaction of seeing the killer or killers punished. We can't guarantee an eye for an eye, sentiment against capital punishment being what it is. Nor can we swear to you on a stack of Bibles that the thieves will be convicted, recent Supreme Court decisions being what they are. But we are not ignoring you, Mr. Prescott, we're not ignoring you or your daughter-in-law. That you can take for gospel."

I studied their faces as Benedict laid it on the line. Shaw looked thoughtful, I thought, but I couldn't be sure because of the sunglasses. Draper's expression was hard to

53

read, but it contained at least a modicum of skepticism. That's the way it is when you level with cop-doubters. They wouldn't believe a policeman if he swore on oath. That's one reason why we don't tell a lot of people the way it is.

I asked a question. "Mr. Prescott, Mrs. Prescott told me that you alone knew the combination to the safe. Fingerprints on it were smudged, probably deliberately by gloved hands. Have you at any time given that combination to anyone else? Your son here, for instance?"

The skepticism changed to scorn. "No one else knew. I destroyed the printed combination once I had memorized it. And if you're hinting that I'd go around telling my safe combination to every Tom, Dick, and Harry, you're barking up the wrong tree."

"But the safe was opened. It wasn't forced."

"It's my opinion that Mrs. Prescott left it open when she last put her jewelry away. I opened it for her, but I didn't stand there and watch her put it in and close it. She's inclined to be careless, anyway."

"Has she ever left it open before?"

"I don't mean open. I would have noticed that. I mean openable. If you don't turn the dial when you shut it, it can be opened right up again. She shut it, all right, but I don't believe she turned the dial."

"Where is Mrs. Prescott?" asked Benedict. "We'd like to talk to her about that."

Shaw answered. "Mother's at La Femme."

"I beg your pardon?" Benedict frowned and I blinked.

"La Femme. It's a beauty shop on Newbury Street. She's gone to have her hair done. We've set the funeral for

54

Thursday. She said she wanted to look her best for visiting hours and such. It may seem callous to you, but I understand it." He removed his glasses so that he could stare at us earnestly. "Women put great store in such things."

"But her hair looked newly done yesterday," I blurted. I had particularly noticed, had compared it with Dorinda's just-plain-combed look.

"That was her wig," said Draper dryly. "It covers a multitude of sins."

"I thought that when a lady had a wig, she didn't have to worry about her own hair anymore." I didn't know anybody who had a wig, but I'd seen some women who needed them.

"That's what they tell you before they get the wig," was Draper Prescott's answer. "But, like all their other little games, it doesn't end up as advertised. She should be back shortly after noon if you want to see her then. But no matter what she tells you, it's clear in my mind that Olivia didn't relock the safe door."

"Doesn't that add up to being quite a coincidence?" asked Benedict.

"Coincidence? You mean, because the burglars came and found the safe open? Maybe, but remember it was open all of three months and anyway, I should think it came as just a bonus for them. They no doubt came prepared to blow it if they had to."

Benedict pushed back his chair and stood. "Perhaps. But I find it interesting that the crime was committed the day before you came home. Last-minute planning, so to speak."

I got up, too. "Could it have been in the newspapers that you were coming home? In the society columns, say?"

Draper Prescott looked scornful again. It was, by far, his best expression. More practice, I guessed. "We're not the type of people who care to have our names in the newspapers. I called a friend this morning, a publisher I know, to make certain that Dorinda's death is properly treated—on the obituary page. Furthermore, I warn you now, I know some of you fellows are headline hunters, I won't have any loose talk about my daughter-in-law with journalists. I want you to pass the word along, too, to make sure that your entire organization understands this."

Benedict drawled, "Now, there, Mr. Prescott, you have something in common with the police. We, too, are not the type of people who care to have our names in the newspapers. We feel it interferes with our efficiency. If you'll tell Mrs. Prescott we'll be back at two, we'll be properly grateful." With that, he took his leisurely departure, me following behind somewhat like Dennehy must have looked trailing me the night before, and trying my best to hide a very non-professional grin.

5

"Knute," said Benedict as we got into the car, "I almost forgot to ask you, do you want to come tonight with me to a seminar on Search and Seizure, Interrogation and Confession?"

He was always going to seminars but he'd never before asked me to come along. I hedged, "Where—and what time does it start?" and he told me eight o'clock at Northeastern University. "I guess it won't do me any harm."

"It's a complicated subject. I'm afraid not everybody understands it."

"I'm not sure I do." I moved out into traffic.

"The key remark is, of course, the warning that a suspect has a right to remain silent."

"Followed by that old cliché from English movies—anything you say can and will be used as evidence against you in court."

Benedict took up the recitation we recently had learned by heart. "You have a right to consult with a lawyer of your own choice before you answer any question and to have that lawyer present while you answer any question. If you are unable to hire your own lawyer and you want a lawyer, a lawyer will be provided for you before you are asked any questions." He whipped a small gray book out of his pocket and looked at it to be sure he was letter-perfect. He read on from the book, "At a minimum an affirmative waiver or a 'yes' answer must be obtained from a suspect to the following two questions: 1. Do you now understand all of your rights which we have just explained? 2. With these rights in mind, are you willing to talk to us without a lawyer to represent you."

"What's the book?" I asked.

"*Police Guide to Search and Seizure, Interrogation and Confession.* By Specter and Katz."

"Where'd you get it?"

"At the bookstore."

"I'd like to get hold of one."

"I'll pick one up for you."

"Thanks." I stopped for a red light. We were on Commonwealth Avenue and up ahead I saw the blue and white cord-clad figure of a meter maid. From where I sat, it looked like Gail Gregg. She was walking our way, checking the meter times, and we were driving in her direction. When we met in the middle of the block, I beeped the horn. She looked up and smiled. She was cute in her meter maid hat with visor, as cute, that is, as a girl can look in a uniform. I decided the reason that she bored me was that she was forever talking shop. "When she joined the Police Department, she got married to the force," I told Benedict.

He didn't say anything. He had a talent for minding his own business but I wanted to talk to somebody. "I figure I'm more than old enough to get married and settle down. When I started going out with Gail, I thought maybe she'd be the one. But she isn't."

Benedict said quietly, "Don't worry about it. It will come. When the time is right and the girl is right."

Traffic began to back up at a light up ahead and we sat, the motor idling. "How did you meet Barbara?"

"We grew up together. Two blocks apart in Brighton. I never had to look for the girl, I had only to wait for the time. She wouldn't marry me after she got polio. It took me a couple of years to convince her that it didn't matter to me, that my motives weren't based on pity."

I nodded slowly. Traffic began to move again and we turned the corner to go into the division lot. "Isn't that Cowan?" I asked suddenly. "What's got into him?" Tall, easygoing Chris Cowan, camera swinging crazily from its strap, was running up the division steps as though he were on fire.

I parked and we slid out of the car on either side simultaneously. Inside the doors, we could hear some kind of commotion going on down the hall from the direction of the office. As we came in, Cowan, standing in the center of the room with his face twisted in rage, was swearing to himself, pulling the phrases up from somewhere deep inside. His mouth curled in revulsion even as he spit them out. "The goddamn punk! The little bastard! Wait until I get my hands on him, the no-good son-of-a-bitch!"

59

Cowan's face worked furiously, tried to form itself into some impossible position before he abruptly turned away, head down. I realized he was crying.

The other guys were standing quietly, embarrassed for him, and I said to Davoren, who was nearest to us, "What the devil goes on?" A phone rang shrilly across the room and Pinkerton, looking solemn for a change, went to answer it.

"It's his kid," Davoren said softly. "Three of them skipped school and held up an MBTA car. The subway boys are bringing them here."

"Jesus," I whispered. "No wonder."

Benedict went over to Cowan and said something I didn't hear. Cowan shook his head like a sore bear and moved away from him. Captain Granger came out of his office and said evenly, "Chris, you can come in here." Cowan turned blindly and followed Granger into his office. The door shut behind them.

We all looked at each other. Benedict, Pinkerton, Dracutt, Blasdell was there, too, and Casey. Then we went to our desks and sat down without saying anything. There wasn't anything to say.

I was taking a phone gripe from a young woman who said her ex-boyfriend was following her around, wouldn't let her alone, when they came in. Two big guys in MBTA uniforms, a pair of Boston patrolmen, and the three kids. They looked to be about fifteen or so. One was tall and sandy-haired, Cowan's kid, it was easy to tell, he looked like his father some. One of the others was dark and quite stocky, his hair grew down around his ears, and the third was a scrawny little guy with a pimply face. The MBTA boys looked as though they'd like to boil the lot in oil.

We all looked at each other again and Benedict went to meet them. I switched my phone call to hold and notified Granger, "Captain, they're here."

"Bring them in," he said gruffly, "and the rest of you keep out."

I gave the group the message by gesture. The kids weren't looking at anybody but they didn't give any indication of shame. They acted like cool kids going into see the principal, that's all I could think of. I pictured Cowan waiting in there for his son and I figured maybe oil was too good for them.

The seven disappeared through Granger's door. Davoren came and stood guard outside. I finished my phone call I'd been holding and informed Miss Helen Thompson that she'd have to come down and file a complaint before we could take any action against Roland Styles.

The patrolmen weren't inside too long. When they came out, Davoren intercepted them and walked them down the hall, talking and listening. We were all waiting for Davoren when he came back.

"How did it happen? How serious is it?" Pinkerton wanted to know.

"They used a couple of black plastic water pistols and pulled a holdup on the Maverick to Atlantic run that goes through the East Boston tube under water. One of them, the thin one, held a 'gun' on the driver, that's one of the MBTA guys in there now; they were a two-car train and the other driver's in there, too. The squatty one held the second 'gun' on the people in the car while Cowan's boy collected the loot. Had a paper bag full of billfolds and

61

lady's change purses when they caught them. The Cowan kid tried to ditch the bag down a sewer grating but it wouldn't go through."

"Water pistols," murmured Casey.

"You'd think you could spot 'em," was Dracutt's observation. "Did they get the guns? They take good prints."

Davoren shrugged. "I guess so. The second driver, the one in the lead car, happened to look back and thought something looked wrong. When he stopped the train, he was out in a flash and took off after the kids. That's how they got them so quick."

"What about the witnesses?" Benedict asked.

"They took them to Central Complaint." Davoren cocked an ear toward Granger's office. "They brought the kids here because of Cowan. The Cowan boy didn't even try to hide the fact that his father is on the force." He shook his head. "Something wrong there."

I couldn't claim Cowan and I had ever been buddy-buddies, but I had known him slightly before we ended up together in Division Two. He'd been graduated from Boston Latin a couple of years before I went there and he'd been a big hero, football, baseball, a four-letter man. So that when I was a green kid, my first year in high school, the hero came back and gave us a pep talk before the big game with Boston English. I remembered that now, a good-looking guy, ages old and completely sophisticated it had seemed to us. He was going to Boston College then and one of the seniors said he was going to marry Mary Murphy when he graduated 'cause they were engaged and I said, 'Who's Mary Murphy?' and he said, 'Just about the prettiest girl you'll ever see' and now it all came back to me, just as if it were yesterday.

Later, too, when I'd begun to think seriously of joining the department, my mother had said, "Oh, isn't that nice Chris Cowan a policeman now?" So that maybe, and maybe not, Cowan was one reason why she hadn't put up a big fuss when I took the Civil Service exam.

"How many children does Cowan have?" I asked Benedict.

"Just the one, I think."

"Boy, that's rough." I felt so damn sorry for Cowan. How could the boy have done this to him?

Benedict nodded, started to say something, but his phone rang. I sat there, trying to put my mind back where it belonged, on the Prescott murder. There wasn't anything any of us could do for Cowan but when something bad happens to one of us, we all feel it. I knew that every man jack there was visualizing juvenile court, the resulting publicity, and, worst of all, the misery in Chris Cowan's heart.

"That was Shaw Prescott," said Benedict hanging up his receiver. "He just got word that his father-in-law is due in on the five o'clock plane from Washington. I told him we'd postpone our visit until Mr. Crewe gets in. I said six o'clock."

"That puts a crimp in the seminar."

"Maybe not. The Prescotts are having visiting hours at the mortuary at seven so we should be able to make it all right. It's important that we talk to him, we've got to find some connection. It may go way back. Her father

63

may have some idea. Old friends from the wrong side of the track."

"Then you're sure she triggered the burglary?"

He shrugged his shoulders. "I feel strongly there has to be something. Because of the timing. They zeroed in on the Prescott house just before the Prescotts returned. I can't believe that's purely coincidence."

A man came in the door, turned toward Granger's office. Davoren admitted him to the inner sanctum. "Attorney for the defense," commented Benedict.

"Harry Phillips." I'd recognized the lawyer. He was an able one. I spent some time staring at Granger's door.

"What about lunch?" I asked Benedict when I came out of my brown study.

"I'll eat downtown." He patted his pocket. "I've got that shopping list to start on."

"Right. I'll grab a bite and come on back. You want to take the car?"

"No. I think I'll go MBTA. It's quicker." He smiled at me. "I know better than to invite you to come along."

And I knew better than to offer to do so. A bachelor, I was learning, missed out on a lot of things, a lot of pleasure and a lot of pain.

I was going down the steps, heading for the coffee shop down the block, when Dolph Smith, his green Alpine hat at its usual angle on his head, nearly ran me down.

"Say hey, Knute." He looked up at me with narrowed eyes. Oh, oh, I thought. He's onto the Cowan boy. Of course.

"When are you going to get a new hat, Dolph?" I needled.

He rolled his eyes up toward his brim. "So what's wrong with this one?" Banter abruptly over, he was all business. "They got the Rapid Transit robbers over here?"

I made like Mickey the Mope. "Don't ask me. I'm one of the peasants."

"Sure you are. I hear tell one of the trio is a son of a —detective."

I took two steps past him thinking which course to follow. Should I appeal to his somewhat latent sense of kindness or give him the no comment bit?

"Look," I said, glancing back at him, "take it easy, will you? I can't tell you anything, you'll have to ask the captain. But you're not going to do anybody any good by playing this up big."

His eyebrows rose. "You think I'm the only garden variety snake in town? So I cut it down to one factual paragraph and the other sheets run banner heads. What does my editor say then?"

I turned away. I had no argument to give him. Once again I felt sick for Cowan. What would this do to his career? And what about the boy's whole life? Why didn't these damn kids think before they acted? I said, "No comment, Dolph," and went off to nibble at a ham sandwich. What the hell, I could afford to lose a few pounds anyway.

By the time I got back, the meeting in Granger's office had broken up. Cowan was missing and, thank God, Dolph Smith had disappeared, too. I just hoped he wasn't on Cowan's back.

A pair of blue-jeaned purse snatchers were sitting sullenly by Pinkerton's desk as he and Dracutt took down particulars. It seemed they'd knocked down an eighty-year-old woman and sent her to the hospital, all for the sake of $6.80 in her pocketbook. I couldn't stand to look at them, they made me sick. As Pinkerton went into the routine of advising them on their rights, I thought, Rights! What about the rights of the rest of us?

6

Benedict and I arrived at the Prescott house promptly at six and found all three Prescotts and George Stanley Crewe dressed in proper dark clothing for the visiting hours to come and waiting for us. It was not until Shaw introduced his father-in-law as General Crewe that I realized who he was. I'd seen his name in the papers upon occasion. He was high up in Pentagon circles. I was struck by the oddness of his eyes. They were a strange tan color and there were dark circles below them. All I could think of was that they looked like the eyes of a man who'd seen everything.

There was an air of the aristocrat about him, not just the look of success, but more than that. And with it, those dead eyes. I couldn't imagine him crying, not for his daughter nor anyone else. Feeling faintly sorry, perhaps, but with the realization that that was the way things go. I wondered what sort of father this man had been.

Mrs. Prescott was being charming. "I wish you could have heard them at the beauty shop, General. Dorie was such a favorite there. They were extending their condolences to me all morning. And, of course, there will be so many friends coming this evening and tomorrow evening. . . ."

"These are some of Boston's finest." Draper Prescott, with his usual grace, had the general's other ear. "They seem more interested in the Prescott family than in looking for murderers."

General Crewe studied us with his world-weary eyes. "She was not the sort of girl one would expect to end up like this," he said in a rich voice, rich but soft, somehow gentle. As though he were used to his every whisper being heeded.

"We're troubled about the timing of the robbery," explained Benedict. "Has there ever been anyone in your daughter's past, someone she knew even casually, who might have ended up in Boston eager to make a dishonest dollar? Someone whom she might have told about this empty house? Innocently, of course."

The general smiled a sad, understanding smile. "Never." The word was definite and the implication was that nothing more need be said.

"Mrs. Prescott, you told me yesterday that you were sure you had shut the safe after last using it," I reminded her. "Are you certain you locked it? Your husband says the dial must be turned to secure it."

"Well, yes, of course. That is, I'm almost certain."

She turned to Draper with a little helpless smile. "It was quite some time ago and I do tend to be careless. . . ."

"Then we can assume that you might not have locked the safe?" I pursued the matter.

Draper Prescott made an impatient gesture. "I told you she didn't lock it. You can take my word for it."

Shaw Prescott was wearing a black armband but the others were not. He fiddled with it now, moving it up an inch, then back down. "Hadn't we better get going? There may be people there early."

"Is there anything else I can tell you?" asked General Crewe in that remarkable voice. Again it made a point, even in the question. It was almost as though he had said, "There isn't anything else I can tell you."

Mrs. Prescott stood up and shook the skirt of her black dress into a proper line. Her own hair, I saw, was more silver than the wig. Both looked good on her, although I thought the wig made her look a little younger.

Benedict and I stood up, too. "Thank you for your time," Benedict said. "We'll report to you as soon as we have any information."

Shaw roused himself from a sort of reverie and came with us to the door. As we passed the art collection in the hall I said, "Funny they didn't steal any of the pictures, the silver, anything like that."

He looked at the walls as though he'd never seen them before. "Why would anyone want them?" he asked. "My parents have abominable taste. Haven't you noticed that?" He watched us go down the walk with the air of a man who had nothing else in the world to do. An odd lot, these Prescotts and Crewes, in my opinion.

As I started the car, I suggested we go by the division before we ate. "It won't take but a minute. There's something I want to check on."

Benedict glanced at me. "Something ring a bell with you?"

"I don't know. It's that beauty shop business. I've heard it mentioned two or three times now and it just occurred to me that maybe there was somebody they met there. Women talk a lot in beauty shops, I'd guess. It's a nutty idea, but it won't do any harm to ask Robbery to check it out." I slowed for the car in front of us to turn, speeded up again.

"A beauty shop," said Benedict thoughtfully. "La Femme. That was the name of it, wasn't it? On Newbury Street?"

"Wouldn't it be interesting if any or all of the women robbed patronized La Femme?"

We exchanged glances. "A beauty shop," murmured Benedict again. His eyes were bright. "We should have an answer by morning." He settled back in his seat. Suddenly I felt clever.

We pulled into Division Two and I said, "I'll be right out. We've still got plenty of time if we have a sandwich."

Benedict nodded and I took off. I got no further than the front doors, though, because Granger was coming out and the look on his face stopped me dead.

"Come on," he ordered. "Cowan's shot himself."

I guess I stared at him but I didn't spend much time doing it. I turned on my heel and was back in the car before he'd reached the sidewalk. "Cowan," I said to Benedict, starting the motor. "He's shot himself."

Benedict opened the door so that Granger could get in. I made the trip to Roslindale in well under ten minutes. Benedict asked one question during the ride. "Is he dead?"

Granger nodded. After that we listened to our own thoughts.

Cowan's place was a single house set in between a couple of two-families. There was a brick wall along the front of it and a patrol car in the drive. As we arrived, so did a police ambulance. We made the door as the stretcher was rolled out.

We didn't know the patrolman who answered the door so Granger identified ourselves. I could hear someone sobbing inside. The officer stood aside and we went in. The living room was on the small side but immaculate. A woman crouched in a chair in the corner, her head bent, her shoulders shaking. She had dark, curly hair with streaks of gray in it. Her figure was ample, she filled the chair. That's all I could see of her, pretty Mary Murphy who had married good-looking Chris Cowan a long time ago.

The ambulance crew came in behind us and the place was full of people. Mrs. Cowan didn't once raise her head. Granger asked the second patrolman, "Where's the boy?"

"He took off."

"Jesus, Mary, and Joseph," said Granger softly. Then he went after the stretcher-bearers to the back of the house. After a moment, Benedict and I went, too.

He'd done it in the garage. The top of his head was missing. The gun, police issue, lay on the floor beside him. Granger picked it up with a pen through the trigger, wrapped it in a handkerchief. He turned, bumped into Doc Albert for the simple reason that he didn't see him. Granger wasn't seeing anything.

Not until the body had been taken away did we go back into the house. A priest had come, Father Kileen, and was talking softly to Mrs. Cowan, who still sat in her corner chair, head bowed. At least the awful weeping had stopped. And, when Granger spoke to her, she raised her head, raised it slowly as if it were very heavy, and looked at us.

She was no longer pretty, and certainly not pretty now, but I could see the traces. A dimple that flashed even when she spoke, big round blue eyes now clouded and aching. I could see the raw grief that glazed Mary Cowan's eyes and I wondered for a minute if she had let go of her mind because her eyes looked as though she had. But she answered Granger all right in a ragged voice; she told him that Maurie, the boy, had left the house after a row with his father. "And then Chris went out into the garage—" Her voice, a sudden balloon, soared and broke. Father Kileen began a prayer and I backed away. It was hard to watch and hard to listen.

"The boy, Mrs. Cowan," Granger persisted gently, "where could he have gone?"

"He's my baby. My baby!" she sobbed.

"To relatives? To friends? Where, Mrs. Cowan? We must find him."

"It wasn't supposed to be this way." She stared now at something unseen, spoke to someone not present. "Happily ever after. Happily ever after. Happily. Ever after." She dug at the arms of the chair. "Did he hate me so?"

Doc Albert came in from the back of the house and told Granger he would give her a sedative. One of the patrolmen reported that something had been bubbling on the stove and that he'd turned the burner off. The priest had his rosary beads out. Mary Cowan began to cry again. No sound this time, just tears and a mouth like a big, changing O.

"The boy," said Granger desperately.

"What did I do?" whispered Mrs. Cowan. "What did I do wrong?" She turned to Father Kileen. "I never miss mass. I've been a good woman. What did I do wrong?" She stiffened. "When my mother was sick and died, that's what it is. We put her in a nursing home. That's what we did wrong. We're being punished, punished!"

"Relatives?" Granger kept on.

"I'm all alone." She clasped her hands together and looked to the ceiling. "Dear God, I'm all alone!"

Doc Albert moved in with his sedative.

Granger came away, defeated. "I'll call Central Complaint and give them the description. Maybe he's gone to one of his pals. They were all let loose on bail this afternoon. Iggy Knotts, that's one, and Doug Elmer." He read off the addresses from his notes and Benedict wrote them down. There was no nonsense about being off duty or missing seminars. As the captain had said, we had to find the boy. The unspoken end of the sentence was before he did anything else.

There was no one at home at the Knotts' apartment,

no one at all, and first-floor tenants seemed to think that the Knotts family had taken off, boy, bag, and baggage, that afternoon late. I copied down the make and year of car, part of a license number. We could fill that in from the registry. We notified Central Complaint to send out the word.

Then we went looking for Maurie Cowan at Doug Elmer's.

Doug, it turned out, was the thin kid with the acne. His father was a larger, thinner copy without the bad skin. There was no Mrs. Elmer, the father told us. "She's been gone a long time." He didn't elaborate.

"No, we haven't seen the Cowan kid around here and he'd damn well better not stick his nose in my door," Mr. Elmer growled. "Bad company, that's what I tell Doug here. You keep bad company and you'll get tarred with the same brush. But what do you expect, him palling around with the son of a cop. Everybody knows cops are sadists, everybody knows that. . . ." I let him ramble on and on. Maybe he didn't consider us cops and maybe he didn't care. Tarred with the same brush. All of us. I was immune to it at that moment. What good did it do to protest? Unloved and unsung. The world upside down. The police were the villains and the villains were lily white. I must inform you of your rights, Mr. Killer, Mr. Mugger, Mr. Rapist, Mr. Thief. To hell with it.

It was after nine when we left the Elmers' empty-handed. "Now what?" I asked Benedict.

He gave me an address and I looked at him in surprise. "I had a word with the Elmer boy while his father was riding his tirade," he explained. "It seems there's a girl."

74

"There usually is," I said glumly and started the car with a roar.

Nancy diSteppano was the name of Maurie Cowan's game and she was built like a pencil with little bumps for breasts and slightly bigger bumps for buttocks. She had on a miniskirt as short as the law would allow and white fishnet stockings encased her little girl legs. Long dark hair hung halfway down her back and she blinked at us through shaggy bangs. Her folks weren't at home and who are you guys, anyway?

We told her. Something flickered behind the bang curtain but the little face that showed stayed expressionless. "We're looking for your boyfriend," I said. "Have you seen him?"

She patted her hair. "I've got a lot of boyfriends. Which one?"

"Maurie Cowan?"

No flicker this time. She was expecting it. "He's no boyfriend of mine."

"Is that so? Doug Elmer says he is."

"That creep."

"Suppose we come in and look around? It won't take a minute." I had a foot in the door.

"I don't have to let you in. I know about those things."

"That's right. But a pretty girl like you doesn't want to give a policeman the wrong idea, does she?"

She arched her flat little chest. "What do you want with Maurie, anyway?"

Benedict answered, sounding kindly like a father. "We want to tell him something has happened to his dad."

Her face went blank. Not just carefully expressionless

but utterly blank. "What's happened to his old man?"

"He's dead." Benedict spoke softly.

"Maurie's father is dead?"

I nodded. "We think he'd want to know."

There was a sudden small sound inside and we all looked toward it. Someone had stepped on a squeaking board.

She glanced back at us, her eyes narrowed. "How'd it happen?"

"That's something we'd rather tell the boy. May we see him?" Benedict edged closer.

She was torn, that was obvious. She was expecting Maurie to say something to let her know it was all right. But, other than the squeak of the board, all was quiet.

"He killed himself, as a matter of fact." Benedict spoke so that anyone in the room beyond could hear.

"Killed himself!" Her mouth dropped and her eyes widened. She dropped her hand from the side of the door and we stepped forward, Benedict saying, "All right to come in?" Then we were inside and Maurie Cowan, standing frozen in the middle of the room, was staring at us with panic-filled eyes.

"You told me you wouldn't let them in," he screamed abruptly at the girl. He wanted to run, was poised to run, he might at any minute.

"But, Maurie, it's your father. They said he's dead." Forgive me, her face, her body, her entire self begged.

"They're lying. They said that just to get in. They're lying. My father's not dead." He attempted to laugh. "If you said I was dead, that I'd buy. He was all set to murder

76

me when I took off. And what he didn't do, these guys will finish."

"He shot himself." I said it roughly to see him bounce. "He took his gun out to the garage and blew his head off."

The color faded from his face and it was, in that fraction of a second, an old face. His mind reached for the reality and worried it. I could almost see the thoughts race in and out until one sunk like a stone and the thought that remained, stayed, forever and forever buried in his subconscious, was "Because of me. He killed himself because of me." If that's what Cowan was trying to get across, he had done it.

We drove Maurie back to his house. Casey and Mrs. Casey were there, planning to spend the night. Mrs. Cowan had been put to bed, Mrs. Casey told us. The sedative was working up to a point, "But she cries a lot in her sleep," said blond, plump Mrs. Casey. They looked at the boy; then, realizing how they looked at him, moved their eyes away.

He hadn't said much on the ride over and now I realized he was shaking. He tried to control it, I could see that by the tense set of his jaw, by the way he bunched his hands. I said, "Mrs. Casey, could you make Maurie here some hot chocolate? You had any dinner, Maurie? I thought not. And a sandwich, please, Mrs. Casey."

"I'm not hungry."

I turned on him, suddenly furious. "So eat anyway." The sympathy bit had swallowed me up for a little while, seeing him recognize his guilt had done it, but now I saw him for what he was. His father had said it. A punk. Because of this nothing, a good man was dead. Not only dead, but dead by his own hand. I shoved the kid toward the kitchen. "Get in there. Sit down. And shut up." Benedict let us go.

After Mrs. Casey produced the food, she went out. Couldn't stand to be around him. I didn't blame her. I sat and stared at him, watched him eat with a kind of perverse pleasure. Picking at the food at first, then gulping. It turned out he was hungry.

"I suppose you want to know why I did it, held up the subway," he said at last. There was chocolate on his mouth. He looked like a surly, dirty-faced baby.

"I don't give a damn why you pulled your stupid caper." I almost spit at him. "I could sing the chorus for you anyway, God knows we've heard it often enough, all of us." I skewered him with my gaze. I was filled with what I had to say and by Jesus he was going to hear it.

"You're all alike, all of you whiny, snot-nosed babies. My parents don't understand me, they want me to go out and act square like they do. They won't let me go and make a hundred thousand mistakes and then bail me out each time. They're idiots from nowheresville. They won't believe that it's okay to smoke pot and they won't give us the right to run this bloody world. So what if we're too young and know nothing. We can do just as well as they did. Sure we lie and steal and do any damn thing we want to. It's a free country, isn't it? Who says they're so pure anyway? Besides, they don't love us!"

My voice had risen to where it was close to shouting and I dragged it down again, but it wasn't easy.

"Who said your parents owed you anything besides doing their best to keep you safe and sane and alive with at least a chance to make it on your own some day? Who said they're supposed to be saints or supermen? And what's this love bit—would you recognize love if it flew up and chewed you on the ear? Your idea of love is give me, give me, give me. And the echo comes back—me, me, me! So tell me no tales, Maurice Cowan, and sell me no bills of goods. You're a big fat zero in my book and if it weren't for my regard for your father and your poor sad mother upstairs, I wouldn't raise a finger to help you out of quicksand."

I got up and left the table then. I didn't look at any of them in the living room. I just walked out and sat in the car in the dark. I was ashamed of myself.

I'd meant every word of it but it was the wrong time and maybe the wrong place. It had poured out of me like vomit and by rights I should have stuck around and tried to straighten things up. He was, after all, only a kid and he'd just lost his father.

But the sight of him made me sick and that wasn't very adult and I wasn't very proud of it.

To tell the truth, sitting out there listening to the sounds of crickets and my own thoughts, it scared me.

7

The morning *Herald-Traveler* treated Cowan's death better than I'd feared and I guessed that Granger had gotten through to somebody. Of course, on the other hand, could be that Dolph Smith had a sense of decency under the brim of that green hat. There was no time set yet for the funeral, I learned when I got into Division Two, but we were going to send a big blanket of flowers as soon as we found out the details. I chipped in to Davoren, who was taking the collection, meanwhile avoiding Cowan's empty desk. Casey's was unoccupied, too. He and his wife were still with Mrs. Cowan, I surmised.

After some fumbling around, we got down to work. I sent in a request marked urgent to Robbery for a quick check on La Femme as it related to the robbery victims, a task I'd failed to get around to the night before. It was a quiet morning, all in all, so Benedict and I took a run by the place just before lunchtime.

It was a whitewashed stucco building set on a corner. There were ornate wrought-iron grilles on the windows of both stories and the view through the glass was obscured by filmy white curtains. The door out front was one of those heavy, carved Spanish-type portals with broad wrought-iron hinges. A fancy gold and white canopy ran out to the curbing to shield milady from the rain. A small brass plaque set into the stucco read modestly La Femme. That was all, no wigs in the windows, no pictures of pretty girls with improbable hairdos. If you didn't know what it was, you might just guess wrong.

"They've confused their nationalities," Benedict commented. "Using Spanish decor with a French name."

We stopped for a few minutes in a loading zone and watched. A woman with swirled silver hair went in leading a gray poodle on a leash. "They do get to look like each other sometimes, don't they?" I asked rhetorically. After a moment, two other women came out, both beautifully dressed, their hair artfully arranged. We watched them march off toward Bonwit Teller.

"Do you suppose it's possible?" I was beginning to have some doubts. "It looks like an expensive place for sure. Why should anybody risk a successful business to burgle houses?"

Benedict shrugged. Three women came and went. Five minutes later, another pair. Every one of them looked well off from head to toe.

"I don't know." I started the car. "It will probably turn out to be a bad steer. Chances are the other victims never set foot in the place." I nodded my head in the direction we were going. "There are dozens of beauty shops on this street alone. Seems to me there's a hairdressing parlor on most every corner."

"Yes, they are plentiful. All the more reason to be interested in whether our particular ladies patronize the same shop." Benedict took out a little pearl-handled knife with a file and began to file his nails. He'd been subdued since our visit to the Cowans'. But then, so had I.

"I was reading a book"—I continued up Newbury Street, there was a nice little restaurant up aways—"written by an ex-policeman. Sort of the psychology of a cop, you know. Some of it was too technical for me, the guy had a couple of degrees, not just an AB, but one of the things it talked about was the number of suicides on the force. It surprised me, I can tell you. If I remember the figures right, it was something like an average rate of twenty-two percent per hundred thousand."

Benedict examined his nails and put his knife-file away. "Did it give a reason?"

"Uh huh. Something he called anomie. It's a neurosis that stems from cynicism." I didn't tell him how cynical I'd been feeling. "Do you suppose that was part of Cowan's reason?"

"Possibly. I imagine, too, that he was as disturbed in his way as the boy is." He sighed. "It's not pleasant to psychoanalyze a friend."

"No. I was out of line last night with Maurie. I should have kept my cool."

He didn't answer and I didn't expect him to, but I wanted to admit that I knew I was wrong. I pulled up in front of the restaurant—miracle of miracles, there was a parking space!—and we had a good lunch.

When we got back to Division Two, the report from Robbery was on my desk.

I read it and passed it over to Benedict. When he was through reading, he said quietly, "I guess we'd better show this to Granger." We went in with it to see the captain.

"So we think it's significant that all three women robbed last weekend were customers of La Femme," I summed up when we'd shown him the report. "Robbery has asked the suburban towns to follow through on this with some of their housebreaks and they've given us an okay to make an investigation, at least tacitly. We just may have hit the jackpot."

"Knute thought of it last night," Benedict put in, "but we didn't get going on it till this morning."

"Let's check the records and see who operates the place. I'll put Davoren on that." Granger was wearing his old beat-up blue suit again and he looked tired. "I agree with you, Knute. Moses on the mountain, you may have stumbled onto something."

"The thing is, I don't know just how to approach an investigation." I'd been thinking about the next move ever since I'd seen Robbery's answer to my question.

Granger looked thoughtful and Benedict nodded.

"If we just barge in there asking questions, we're not going to find out a thing. We need somebody on the inside of the place to snoop around. And neither Benedict nor I are the type."

Granger pulled on his lower lip. "A woman. Obviously."

"Yes. But not just a customer, especially a strange one. If it's a legitimate beauty shop, and we can assume it is or women like Mrs. Prescott wouldn't go there, then a strange customer can't go prowling around enough, can't ask enough questions without telegraphing the punch line. Especially if somebody in there has something to hide."

"You mean, we need someone to work at La Femme?" Benedict looked interested. "Yes, that would be helpful."

"Yeah, but where are we going to find someone we can trust who has the added ability to work in a beauty salon?"

"I don't think it necessarily has to be a woman. Barbara tells me a lot of the hairdressers today are men."

I made a face. "I don't think any guy on the force could turn hairdresser on the side. We haven't even got an amateur barber."

"One of the meter maids?" suggested Granger.

"Maybe. If she could legitimately get a job. But they have licenses like a barber, don't they? I mean, you just can't walk in and claim you've had experience. . . ."

Granger rang for Davoren. "Suppose we post a notice on the bulletin board. It could be that one of them had aspirations to be a beauty operator."

"It won't hurt to try," Benedict agreed. "And if not here, then the other divisions."

"If it doesn't work, I have another idea." They waited and I went on. "Not as good, but better than nothing. There's this woman in Wellesley, a neighbor of the Shaw Prescotts. She's a kind of a kook, just the type that would go to La Femme I'd think, only she doesn't. That is, I don't think she does. Anyway, she's the oddball kind of

85

woman who's honest and smart. I'll bet if anyone in the customer category could get any information out of La Femme without arousing suspicion, Kay-Kay Mason could."

"Who?" Granger looked startled.

"Kay-Kay Mason. I know it's a silly name, but she's okay. Well, most of the time I think she'd be okay. She does hit the bottle. I wrote her up in the Wellesley report."

Granger remembered. "I don't like the idea of trusting an alky. . . ."

"I know. But I honestly don't think it's gone all the way. I just think she's on the verge."

"I thought she was an older woman." Granger spoke ruminatively.

I felt the edges of my ears burn. I hadn't expected the captain to make cracks about my so-called Casanova status. "So?" The word might have been insulting only I took just a little of the edge off it.

"All right," said Granger. "We'll try it both ways." He directed Davoren, who had entered while we tried Kay-Kay Mason and found her not entirely wanting, to post a notice for the meter maids and he gave me the okay to ring in Kay-Kay if I could. With the warning to keep a close tab on her.

I got her phone number from information and dialed it. It rang several times and I thought she was out, one way or another, but just as I was about to hang up, she answered.

"Mrs. Mason, this is Detective Severson. I came to see

you the other evening, remember? About Dorinda Prescott." I heard the dog yapping in the background.

"Yes, of course. Be quiet, Pujums!"

"I wonder if I could see you this evening. I want to ask you a favor. An official favor."

"Oh, dear. I'd planned to go to Dorie's wake this evening."

"Maybe I could meet you there. It's at Waterman's, isn't it?"

"Yes. I thought I'd go in early. Right after seven."

"I'll be there. We can go someplace and talk afterward."

"All right. I'll wait for you." She hung up and I rang Granger to give him the word. "And she sounded cold sober," I added.

"That shop is owned by Herman Agnew," he told me.

I was surprised. "But he's a building contractor. Highways, houses, office buildings, big kind of stuff."

"I guess it goes under the heading of diversification. You could find that out when you go to see him."

"Right. One thing sure, he couldn't be fronting a burglary operation."

"Davoren set up a date with him for you tomorrow morning at ten. You can give him a pitch about hiring our ringer, too, if we find one. His executive offices are in the Prudential Building. Oh, by the way, Cowan's funeral is set for Saturday morning. Casey called in, said Mrs. Cowan was taking it better now. We'll all go, of course, except for a skeleton crew. We're planning on a full contingent from all divisions."

"What time?"

"It's a Solemn High Mass of Requiem at nine. They won't bury him in the proper part of the Catholic cemetery, but when you've given your best to the church they'll find a corner for you. Which is good. We'll meet at the funeral home at eight-thirty. All go in together."

I made a note of the time and address and added a memo of Herman Agnew's office at 10:00 A.M. "Mrs. Prescott's funeral is tomorrow," I reminded Granger. "Think there's any point in going as an observer?"

Granger thought a minute. "No. I don't think so. If anybody shows up from that beauty shop, I don't want them to get the wind up. They could conceivably go out of respect to the family, so on the surface of it, it wouldn't mean anything. We could conceivably go because she died a violent death, but a guilty man doesn't always see things logically and I don't want to take the chance. It might do harm rather than good."

I nodded at the telephone. I didn't like funerals much anyway and God knew I saw enough of them. "What about this wake tonight? Had I better meet Mrs. Mason outside?"

"I'd say so. I don't want to flush any birds. Not when we could catch our limit later on."

I nodded again and that was why I sat in my car just outside of Waterman's and waited for Kay-Kay Mason. I came early so as not to miss her and, since it was still light out, I had a good view of the people going in and out.

I saw the Prescotts and General Crewe arrive. They drove their Cadillac in back where parking was provided for the family. They sat stiffly, eyes straight ahead. I didn't think they noticed me at all.

Shortly after seven, people began going in. Men and women of various ages, all of them well dressed and solemn. The proper face for the proper occasion, the proper dark clothes. Except, perhaps, for a young fellow in a tan silk suit cut along modish lines, and Kay-Kay Mason. She had on a shocking pink outfit that would literally stop traffic. I called out to her and she turned, looked around, then came over to the car. I noticed a couple of gents passing by swivel their heads for a second look.

"I'll wait out here," I told her. She looked as though she never touched a drop.

"Cloak and dagger stuff."

"Not really. Quieter this way. Less attention paid. Except for that dress." I grinned at her. "Hard to miss that."

She looked down at her outfit. "I don't believe in mourning. I liked Dorie all right. I want to show up to say I'm sorry. But I won't wear black for anybody." She glanced toward the funeral home. More visitors were going in. "I won't be long."

"Take your time." I watched her go up the steps. An elderly gentleman nearly fell over his own feet opening the door for her. I sat and watched people, listened to the traffic sounds from Kenmore Square. The Red Sox were playing at Fenway Park. I wondered if they really could win the pennant. Last year, they'd been in ninth place, now they were hot in contention. What a difference a year makes.

"Well, that's over with." Kay-Kay had come up to the

car without me seeing her. "I'll bring you back to pick up your car," I told her. "I know a little place where we can have dinner while we talk. You haven't eaten yet, have you?"

She shook her head and then arched her eyebrows at me. "Not afraid of being seen with an ancient in public?"

"No, ma'am. If you're referring to yourself, I'm sure not."

She laughed like a girl. "I must say you're good for my ego, Detective Severson."

I took her to Mother Anna's, where the pasta is heavenly and cooked to order so it takes longer. I reflected that she was one of the few women I'd ever met whom I enjoyed being with, without having romantic notions. That amused me somehow. They gave us a booth in the corner and when we'd ordered a drink, I began my pitch.

"You were the one who put the idea in my head," I preambled. "You said something about Dorie Prescott going to a fancy beauty shop. Then I discovered that both she and her mother-in-law patronized a place called La Femme on Newbury Street. Ever heard of it?"

"I think so." She looked thirstily at the waiter as he put the drinks on the table. "Rather posh, isn't it? I've never been there. I go to Mr. Richard's in Wellesley. He's a nice little fellow."

"Would you switch to La Femme for a time or two? It's important."

"I suppose so. But I don't understand why." She was halfway through her drink already, I noticed. I tried to get the waiter's eye. They were busy in Mother Anna's and I knew Kay-Kay would want another.

"We've found that several women who've been robbed go to that beauty shop. It might just be a coincidence, but . . ." I managed to get the waiter's attention and I signaled a repeat order.

"You think someone at that shop is passing out information? The lady most likely to have a houseful of goodies, is that it?" Her eyes sparkled.

"Something like that. We could go in officially and ask questions, but we don't think we'd get very far. It takes a woman, one who's bright enough to ask idle questions and get busy answers."

"Thanks for the compliment." She downed the rest of her martini just as the waiter produced another round. "What questions do you want me to ask?"

"Not so much ask, as notice. The attitude, the atmosphere, the type of clientele and the sort of personnel. If anything comes up that might be interesting, well, it would be up to you to take it from there."

She picked up her new drink, toasted me with it. "Sounds like fun."

"I don't believe there's any danger. Just don't look too prosperous. And don't give them your address. It will be useful to find out if they ask for it."

"The Girl from UNCLE, slightly over-ripe. That's me." She smiled brightly. She was enjoying the prospect. She was a pretty cool character, I thought she could bring it off if anybody could. But, unless we could find another in, it might take forever. I had a sudden thought. "It's ex-

91

pensive, I think. If you want it, I'll try to come up with the fee."

She gave me a roguish smile. "I think I can afford it. You really are rather a doll, Detective Severson, and since I'm almost old enough to be your mother, I can say that. Are you married? Do you have children?"

I shook my head and finished my first drink. I was way behind her, in more ways than one.

"I wish I had a daughter, then," Kay-Kay Mason told me. "I'd sic her on you so fast she'd make your head spin."

I changed glasses, raised the second one to her. "And if she were anything like her mother, I'd be a dead duck." We laughed and I didn't even feel mawkish playing the gallant. Pretty soon we ate spaghetti with clam sauce and I took her back to her car practically sober.

I helped her in and was closing the door, when she stuck her head out the window to look at me.

"Thanks," she said.

"My pleasure. Mother Anna's isn't the Ritz, but the chow is out of sight."

"That, too, but that's not what I meant. I meant, thanks for asking me to do something useful." She drew her head back in and started the motor. Over the sound of the engine, I heard her last words on the wind. "It's nice, for a change."

8

Before I went to bed that night, I boned up on my homework while Mein Hair, the true Casanova of the Severson ménage, went out tomcatting. The gay life of the eligible bachelor, I thought wryly while taking notes on the latest figures on burglaries in the city of Boston. Up from 2,386 the first six months of 1966 to 2,593 the first six months of 1967. A man like Herman Agnew, I thought, would be inclined to be skeptical when I put it to him that one of his enterprises might house a den of thieves. There's nothing a businessman likes better than facts and figures. When I entered his offices at five minutes of ten the next morning, I had plenty of ammunition. I was going it on my own, Benedict was holding the fort at Division Two, which, God knew, was short-handed.

Agnew's offices were all pale paneling and thick gold carpets. His secretary looked pretty New Yorkish by Boston standards. I gave her my name and she commanded me to be seated. The chairs in the reception room were contoured of black leather in strange shapes. I sat in one and found it more than comfortable, almost seductive.

"Mr. Agnew will see you now, Detective Severson," the secretary told me at exactly ten o'clock. I forced myself out of my affectionate chair and walked in through double ivory-colored doors into a four-window office with a desk the relative size of a battleship. A big, bulky man with a face like an Irish bricklayer's sat behind it.

He stood up, not to a very great height, and reached over the expanse of desk to shake my hand. "Sit down, Severson," said Agnew cordially enough. "What can I do for you?"

Another black leather chair held me as I began my preamble about La Femme. I approached the meat of the matter cautiously. "We're interested in a beauty shop called La Femme. We understand you're the owner."

He nodded. His hair had been red once, I guessed. Now it was rusty, touched with gray.

"We have reason to believe one of your employees there, if not more, is cooperating with a gang of housebreakers." I waited for his reaction.

"What makes you think that?"

I told him. Somehow it sounded lamer than ever, so I went over it a couple of times. "In my line of business we learn to trust in hunches. I'll grant you that's all this is."

"Sounds like one of those 'biggest crimes of the century' movies," commented Agnew. He was waiting to be convinced, waiting patiently.

94

"The average citizen may not be aware of the sharp rise in thefts in recent years. Every thief, from pickpocket to tailgater, has been working overtime, it seems, and while we catch our share, the public itself seems to be doing its damnedest to make things tough. Take banks, for instance. It used to be that the teller was protected by bulletproof glass, bars, and high counters. Now banks have done away with all that, look more like somebody's big living room than a bank."

Agnew nodded. "I know I get a lot more pilferage on jobs. I've hired watchdogs for some of my night watch-men."

"This crime at Prescott's started out as a burglary. To be technical, burglary is breaking and entering a dwelling in the nighttime with the intent to commit a felony. Burglaries carry higher penalties than simple breaking and entering, which is what we call forcible entry not necessarily including theft, because a higher degree of fear is involved in breaking into a home than in breaking into a business or a store, especially if it's at night."

"Tailgating, you mentioned that, is hijacking a truck, isn't it?"

"Tailgating is stealing from parked trucks. Hijacking is stealing truck and all. Robbery, as a general term, means stealing, using violence or the threat of violence, and can be armed or unarmed. It carries the highest penalties, up to life imprisonment, of all forms of theft. Larceny, on the other hand, is stealing by stealth rather than by force, the simplest form of stealing with the lowest penalties. Included in this category is purse snatching, unless the victim is threatened, knocked down, or put in fear, in which case the crime is robbery. Other forms of larceny are pickpocketing and shoplifting."

"And you think somebody at La Femme is putting the finger on rich women for a bunch of burglars?" He considered the proposition. "I can't tell you it isn't so. I don't know any of those people other than Margot Kline. I hired Margot to run the place, after that she did the hiring and I don't even know their names, although I've got a record of them, of course." He buzzed for his secretary and smiled a businesslike smile for me. "Miss Gaynor," he said into the intercom when she had responded, "bring me anything you have on La Femme of Newbury Street, will you?" He clicked off the switch. "You've probably wondered why Agnew Enterprises puts its money in a beauty parlor. It's very simple. The building came into my hands and I looked around for its most profitable use. The experts I hire suggested a woman's shop of some kind because of the area and for a while I thought I'd lease it to the first comer. But I set my price high and there were no takers. Then I ran into Margot Kline and she had the beauty shop background, so I put up the dough, she put up the know-how and the management." Again the small smile. "It's worked out pretty well. Ah, thank you, Miss Gaynor." He accepted a file from his secretary and began to look it over.

Miss Gaynor went out and I wrote Margot Kline, after asking the correct spelling, in my notebook.

"There are fifteen regular employees at La Femme," Agnew told me, reading from his folder. "Miss Kline has six male hairdressers, four women hairdressers, two manicurists, two receptionists, and a maid."

"Could I have their names, please?"

He grinned at me, a real grin this time, and passed me the sheet of paper. I read, "John Keith, professional name, Mr. Keith; Val Cesare, professional name, Mr. Valentine; Julio Conti, professional name, Mr. Dante; Robert Ogden, professional name, Mr. Alexandre; Harold Finch, professional name, Mr. Kenneth; Joseph Grebe, professional name, Mr. Joseph."

I looked up for an explanation.

"As I get it," said Agnew, "it's something like going on the stage. They pick fancy names because the women like them and can remember them. It adds to their following."

"Haven't I heard of Alexandre and Kenneth?" It seemed I'd seen ads or read that Jackie Kennedy went to one, something.

"They're not THE Mr. Alexandre or Mr. Kenneth. Margot tells me every shop likes to have one or the other. It sounds like the real thing. Although I imagine the famous ones are actually named Sam Smith or Tom Jones."

I copied off the names carefully and went on to the women listed. No professional names there. Gloria Toner, Pauline Herring, Louise Rock, Renee Taglio, Alice Blair, Martha Elkins, Helen Deal, Betty Munster, Tillie Fields. The first four were hairdressers. Alice Blair and Martha Elkins were receptionists, Helen Deal and Betty Munster were manicurists and Tillie Fields was the maid. The addresses of all were listed, too. I spent a good ten minutes putting it all down so I could read it later.

"What do you want me to do?" asked Agnew when I'd finished.

"We'd like to have somebody in there we can trust," I said. "This Margot Kline, could you vouch for her?"

He got up and went to a window, looked out on the city. "I should be able to say yes. She's been my mistress for two years." He turned and looked at me. "But I've lived long enough to know that anything can happen."

I tried to get it straight. "You mean, you think she could be in on this?"

He shrugged and looked back to the window. "She's greedy. She makes good money and I take pretty good care of her, but she's greedy."

There was no use in asking about any of the others. He'd said he didn't know them. "If we can find a girl who'll fit in, could we put someone in the shop?"

Agnew came back to his desk. "I don't know why not. I tell Margot to hire her, she hires her."

"Could it be done so she wouldn't be suspicious?"

"If the girl is capable. She doesn't have to be an expert, just capable. I can say she's related to a business associate, Margot will buy that. But Margot knows, better than anyone else maybe, that I'm no fool. If you stick a know-nothing in there, she'll wonder."

I sighed and closed my book. "We'll see what we can do."

"Just call Miss Gaynor if you find someone. I may not be around, I expect to be out of town the next few days. She'll have her instructions."

I climbed out of the black leather chair to offer my hand. "Thanks for your cooperation."

He looked slightly surprised. "Why? It's good business."

"Some people haven't figured that out." It was easy to see why Herman Agnew was rolling in money. The only thing was, I wasn't sure I envied him. Ice water is very nice to drink but warm blood in the veins is, in my humble opinion, the perfect solution.

When I got back to the office, I found that Gail Gregg, of all people, had volunteered to work at La Femme. "She went to beautician's school." Granger looked pleased as punch. "I put in a call to the licensing board and got permission for her to operate as a hairdresser. She says at least she can shampoo, things like that. If you set up a deal with Agnew, we're in."

"I did." I might have expected it. Nobody was more gung ho than Gail. I didn't know she'd studied the business. Could be she'd told me about it and it didn't sink in, but no matter. I had to admit to Granger, "If there's anything funny going on there, she'll smell it out."

"Yes, she's a very capable girl." Well, that's what Agnew had specified. A capable girl. But Granger wasn't through. "I want you to hang around, though. Pick her up at night maybe. You can pose as the devoted boyfriend. She can take care of herself, I know, but there's no sense in taking chances."

I hid a grimace. "I'll notify Agnew's secretary. When do you want Gail to go in?"

"See if she can pay a visit this afternoon, tomorrow morning at the latest, for a job interview. She can look around. We want her to start as soon as possible. Happily, the burglars haven't made a hit since Sunday. But you can't ever tell."

"Aren't they weekend golfers? More people away on weekends. Makes the going easier."

"Tomorrow," said Granger, "is Friday."

"I see what you mean. Where's Benedict? He wasn't at his desk."

"He asked me if he could go down to Juvenile Court with Maurie Cowan."

"Oh. What do you think the judge will do with them?"

"Can't say. It's a first offense. I wish I knew the best way to treat first offenders. If I did, I might have gone far in the department." He smiled at me ruefully. "I guess you know I'm up to the twenty-five year mark, just about."

"That long? Congratulations. Are you going to pick up your marbles or hang around?" After twenty years, we could take a pension and move on if we so wished. I hadn't thought about Granger leaving; he'd always been there and I'd simply assumed he always would be.

"I haven't decided." He swiveled his chair around so that he wasn't facing me. "I had an appointment for a job the other day, the day Cowan . . ." He let that sentence trail off. "I had to bypass it."

So that was the reason for the Glen plaid suit. "What kind of job?"

There was a pause. "Bank guard."

I didn't say anything.

"I know." He swung around to me once more. "You know, too, don't you? The choices? Bank guard, night watchman, mail room clerk, or messenger."

"Then why go?"

There was an even longer pause. Granger made a pyramid with his hands, stared down at his desk. After a while, he said slowly, "Some days . . . I get . . . awful tired."

I drove Gail over to La Femme in the middle of the afternoon. I wished like hell I could go in with her, I had a strong feeling that I could just look around the place and know something. "See if this Kline woman will introduce you around," I told Gail. "I'd like a thumbnail sketch of every one of them."

She patted my arm. "I'll do my best." I slowed the car and she got out while I drove on, looking for a parking place. I watched her in the rearview mirror as she moved toward the Spanish door. She looked perky in a beige and brown knit suit.

I parked and waited in front of an art shop of some description where the only ornament in the window, if you could call it an ornament, was a headless figure standing on what would have been its head had it had one, legs waving in the air. It looked as though it had been made of papier-mâché and covered with little tiny pieces of foil. I tried to reason what you would do with it if you had it. I hadn't come up with a single idea when Gail, searching along Newbury Street, found the car and got into it.

"How did it go?" I asked.

"I start in the morning." She glanced at me sideways. "Have you seen that Margot Kline?"

"No. What does she look like? Did you meet the rest of them?"

She cleared her throat. "Margot Kline is, I would say, somewhat unusual-looking. She's probably about thirty years old, five foot seven or eight inches tall, weight around a hundred and twenty-five, maybe a little more. Her hair is red, auburn actually, I think it's dyed, but it's a good job." She glanced again at me.

I played the game the way she expected it. "Wow," I said, "are there any more at home like her?"

I didn't try to analyze the look she gave me. "Would you settle for a capsule description of the ones I remember? There's the beard, he's a fellow named Joseph, Mr. Joseph, they call him. Then there's the shiek, slick black hair, Mr. Dante. Can you believe it? Mr. Valentine is something, he's got great big blue eyes like a baby. Alexandre and Kenneth are more like store dummies than men, one blond-haired, the other wavy brunette. The women are all pros, not young, they look somewhat alike in those white uniforms. Two frozen pusses at the reception desk, a pair of long-fingernailed manicurists, I guess they have to advertise their own service, and a little colored maid who brings coffee and so forth to the customers. That's first impression. I'll fill you in more after I've been there a day or so."

"I didn't know you knew anything about beauty shops. Are you sure they won't catch on?"

"They would if it weren't for the setup. The men are the hair stylists. The women do the shampoos, hand them rollers, mix up the bleaches, donkey-stuff. I can do that all right. La Kline was as nice as pie. She said Mr. Agnew had recommended me. I got the idea they were looking for help anyway."

"I'd give anything if I could do some prowling in that place." I got ready to leave my parking place.

Gail laughed. "You'd feel like a fish out of water. It's all white and gold and French blue. The women change their clothes when they come in, wear a kind of smock thing that sometimes gapes, but the men don't do any looking."

Traffic cleared and I edged out. "On the limp wrist side?"

"Yes and no. It's just a different world. I won't pass on judgments on their sex lives until I know them better. Are you going back to division?"

"Yes. I want to find out what happened with the Cowan boy. Do you want to go back? I assumed you did."

"I guess so. I can take my uniform home and get it cleaned. I won't be needing it for a few days at least." She fumbled in her handbag. "Have you got a cigarette?"

"Sorry."

"That's right. You don't smoke. Here's a crumpled one in the bottom of my bag." She lit the cigarette, exhaled smoke. "Are you mad at me, Knute?"

"No. Should I be?"

"You haven't called lately."

"I'm sorry, Gail. I was on nights, you know, and since we've gone back on days things just haven't worked out."

She smiled at me kindly. "That's okay. I was only kidding. But I would like to invite you to dinner tonight if you're not busy. I've made chicken cacciatore. Made it yesterday and it's perfect the second night."

My mouth watered. I was crazy about chicken cacciatore and my own cooking hadn't been so great lately. What did I have to lose? Gail was a good kid. Cute-looking and plain as an old shoe. "I think I can make it. What time?"

"About seven? Oh, I hope you don't mind. I've got a new roommate. But she'll only be around a few minutes if at all. She's very popular. Goes out just about every night."

I shrugged. One roommate more made no difference to me. I had reached the point where I could take women or leave them and that point, I decided, was a good spot to be.

9

Maurie Cowan and his confederates were given suspended sentences and placed on two years' probation. Benedict looked tired, I thought, when he told me. I'd come to realize that he suffered most when he was dealing with young people in trouble and, while I admired him for it, I couldn't quite follow in his footsteps. I'd decided I wasn't mature enough myself to be objective and therein lay another set of worries—why wasn't I mature enough? Still, I was glad about the Cowan boy. He had a second chance if he could handle it. But one day he'd find out what a police record means. One day, when he'd pretty well forgotten about the rest of it, the motives, the emotions, the very climate of these days, it would hang up there like an ugly smoke signal and there wouldn't be one damn thing he could do about it.

Now I was glad that I'd accepted Gail's invitation to

dinner. It saved me from sitting down in my worry den and stewing about what was going on with Knute Severson. I hadn't seen my folks in weeks, hadn't even called them. Somehow, I didn't want to talk to them. I was showing misanthropic tendencies and I knew it. I knew, too, that I should look only to myself for the reasons but I couldn't recognize them. It was as though I'd lived in a place where the scenery had always been pretty, only one morning I woke up and everything looked ugly. I needed some strange angel to pull me out. Some strange angel, indeed! I snapped my bath towel at Mein Hair, who hissed at me in sport. "Too many nights alone," I told him. He yawned.

I aimed the towel at the rack in the bathroom but missed. It was okay. Thelma was coming tomorrow to clean the place. Good old Thelma, my intrepid cleaning woman. I needed a vacation, that was it. Only, I wasn't due a vacation. I needed a blowup or a wingding or an all-night orgy or . . . I needed to go to Gail Gregg's to dinner. It was time.

Gail lived on Revere Street in a pretty nice apartment. The rent was on the high side and, as a result, she had to have an apartment mate to share the expenses. Her last one had been a husky, healthy female, a physical ed teacher, who was always hanging around. Could be that was one reason why Gail and I hadn't hit it off so well. Now that she had a new roommate who was "out all the time," things might be different. I rang her doorbell with a certain amount of anticipation.

A strange girl opened the door. I stared at her.

"Oh, hi. You must be Knute Severson. I'm Patricia Drake, Gail's new roommate. Come in."

I walked in. Gail was setting the round dining table at one end of the big room. I noticed there were flowers and candles in the middle of it.

"Hi, Knute. Have you and Pat introduced yourselves? Would you pour him a drink, Pat? I've got something crucial in the oven."

"Certainly. Gail's mixed martinis, Knute. I presume that's your specialty?" She twirled the stirrer in a martini pitcher and poured liquid out into a glass. I said, "Thanks," when I took it from her.

"Sit down. Gail will be right out. I may have to leave you in a minute. I thought you were my friend when you rang the bell."

"Thanks." I sat down on the sofa. She sat down across from me. The skirt of her dress was swirly and short, it draped itself gracefully along the legs of the chair.

I took a sip of the martini and cleared my throat. "Are you new to Boston, Miss Drake?"

"Patricia. Or, Pat is even better." She smiled. "Not really. I'm a native but I've been away. I was born and raised in Newton."

I smiled back. The martini glass was cold between my fingers. "So was Robert Morse."

"Robert Morse? Oh, yes, from *How to Succeed in Business.* Do you know him?"

I shook my head. "Do you?"

"No." We both smiled. "Isn't it a small world?" This time we laughed. My laugh was nervous, hers sounded polite.

Gail came in again. She looked very nice in some kind of long, colorful pajamas. "Like my hostess culottes?" She turned like a model. "I've been dying to wear them but I haven't been hostessing lately." She came over and got herself a martini. "Won't you have one, Pat? I meant for you to help yourself."

"No, thanks. Charles will be along any minute."

Gail raised her eyebrows. "Oh, it's Charles tonight, is it?" She grinned at me. "This girl puts out the standing room only sign. The line stretches all the way to the Common."

"Don't be silly, Gail." She tossed her head. Her hair was an unusual color and she wore it shoulder length. "Charles and Leo and Terry are old friends."

"Yes, ma'am! And such handsome old friends."

Patricia Drake's smile grew a little forced. "Please don't. You make it sound so . . ."

"I'm sorry, Pat." Gail, pajama legs swishing, went over to her roommate. "I was just being green with envy. Forgive me."

"There's nothing to forgive." The smile was genuine now. "I'm just edgy. You must forgive me." At that moment, the doorbell rang and Pat was out of her chair and off toward it before Gail could get back to the sofa.

"Come in, Charles," I could hear her voice from the foyer. "I want you to meet Gail's friend. Knute, this is Charles Feeney. Knute is Knute Severson, Charles. He's a detective."

"Really?" I stood up and my hand was grasped firmly by a guy who looked like Joe Harvard and nobody else, except that he looked like Joe Harvard five years hence.

"I'm in stocks," he told me to even things up. "Henneman, Henneman, and Henneman."

"Nice to know you," I said. He towered over me. I figured his height at maybe six-six. "I thought you might be with the Celtics."

Charles, Alias Joe Harvard, laughed. He had neat white teeth. "I played some in college. All set, Pat?"

"I'll get my coat." She went to the closet.

"You're going to the new play?" asked Gail. "I hope it's good."

"I do, too. I voted for the movies. But this woman is culture-happy." He helped Pat on with her coat. He did it with finesse.

"Nice to meet you," he told me.

"My pleasure," I answered.

"See you later," said Gail.

"I hope I'll see you again soon." Pat smiled. We all smiled and nodded and then they were gone and Gail and I sat down again.

"Don't you think she's interesting-looking?"

"Very."

"She's nice, too. She's a widow, you know. That's why she got kind of upset when I was teasing her about the fellows. She says they're not beaux, just old friends. Of her husband." Gail waved her arm in the direction of one of the bedrooms, apparently Pat's. "She keeps her husband's picture beside her bed."

"What happened to him?"

"Vietnam. Last year. Ready for another martini?"

"Yes, thanks. That's tough. Does she work?"

"Oh, yes. She's very bright. She's in an advertising

agency. Mayerheim and Fiske, she writes copy for them. You know, like the girl who cares wears whatsis." Gail manipulated the martini pitcher and I began to relax.

"How did you find her?"

"I advertised. Isn't that funny? But I did; I ran an ad in the paper and she called me up. She said she'd like to live with someone compatible and could we meet and talk it over and here we are. Oh, I almost forgot something else in the oven. Sit a minute, I'll be right back and then I'll talk stream of consciousness about my impressions of La Femme and maybe you can get an idea out of it. . . ."

When she had gone into the other room, I put down my martini glass and let out a long breath. I'd believed that little old ladies in white tennis shoes sitting in small rooms with shawls over their shoulders and fat cats in their laps invented the asinine phrase "love at first sight." I'd believed that until now. I'd believed it until I'd rung the doorbell of this apartment this night. I couldn't even describe her, the color of her hair, the color of her eyes. I hadn't seen her that clearly. It was all I could do not to get up and walk into that bedroom and look at that picture she kept beside her bed. It was all I could do to keep from getting up and going after Joe Harvard and hitting him right in his nice white teeth. It was all I could do to get through that evening, being nice to Gail, eating her carefully prepared dinner, and listening to her pleasant but meaningless chatter. If I'd been miserable before I came there, I was twice as disturbed now. Patricia. Pat Drake. Some strange angel. You can say that again!

I talked about her to Mein Hair. He wanted to go out,

but I wouldn't let him. "She's not very tall," I told him, stroking his stomach. "She's slim and dainty, she moves quick. She's all gold and silver and ivory. There's something about her mouth and the curve of her cheekbone. . . ."

The cat stared at me with inscrutable eyes. I shook my poor head. "I know you don't understand. I guess one girl cat is like another to you and I'll admit I operated somewhat on the same principle."

Mein Hair stood up and stretched, meowed to go out. I took my hand away from him and said, "All right. All right. I get the message." While I was opening the door, I gave about ten seconds to wondering if Gail knew, if I'd hurt her feelings. I didn't want to hurt her feelings and I was pretty sure I hadn't. I'd just been quieter than usual and I hadn't even kissed her good night because that would have been insulting, but she hadn't acted put out, not at all. Which meant that I'd pulled it off without suspicion. Only, she'd know sooner or later, of course, because I intended to telephone Mayerheim and Fiske as early as possible tomorrow morning and when I did, what was I going to say to her, there was the rub, what was I going to say to Pat Drake when I heard her voice coming across that telephone?

I thought of a dozen things and each one sounded phonier than the last. I lay in bed, tossing and turning, beginning conversations. "Pat, somebody happened to give me these tickets to the theater and Gail mentioned how much you like . . ." "Pat, Gail and I have been friends for some time and I don't want you to get the wrong idea, we're just friends. . . ." "Gail mentioned that your office is near ours and since it's raining, I wondered if I could give you a lift home. . . ." how the hell did I know whether it would be raining?

I groaned and turned over on my back. It wouldn't have been quite so tough if I hadn't been seeing Gail. I could just call her up and ask her out on the assumption, the true assumption, that I was interested in taking her out. Interested! But what would she think? That I was Gail's property. That's what she'd think. Well, I'd simply have to explain to her that I wasn't. And to do that I'd have to get her to go somewhere where I could explain. That's all there was to it. That's what I'd have to do. I kept saying it over and over again until I finally went to sleep, maybe about two or three o'clock in the morning.

I felt terrible.

"Benedict," I said as soon as I got in next morning, "what's the best play in town now?"

He looked mildly surprised. "Well, it's early in the theater season, there aren't too many yet. I guess *Keep It in the Family* with Maureen O'Sullivan might be the best chance. I understand it's hard to get tickets, though."

"Great. That's just the thing. Where can I get tickets?" I wasn't too up on obtaining tickets. When I used to go to the theater with Susie Darren, she always picked up the tickets.

Benedict's expression changed to amusement. "What I usually do is try the box office. If they haven't any, try the ticket agencies. You pay a premium, but they may be able to provide you with a pair. What's up? Visiting firemen?"

"Why does it have to be visiting firemen? Can't a guy

develop an interest in the theater?" Without meaning to, I snapped the words.

He looked at me for a minute and I said, "Sorry, Benedict. You didn't know the toe you stepped on had a sensitive corn."

His phone rang and he smiled before he picked it up. "Good luck," he said. "Division Two, Detective Benedict. Yes, sir. Where did you say your car was parked . . . ?"

I got the last two ducats from the theatrical ticket agency, or so the girl told me. They cost plenty, being orchestra and for Saturday night and all but what did I care? I didn't even wait till I got back to the office to call Mayerheim and Fiske, but dialed from a public phone booth. A fat little lady with a bulging shopping bag glared at me through the glass all the while I talked.

"Mrs. Drake? Pat? This is Knute Severson. We met last night. Remember?"

She said what I knew she'd say. "Oh, yes, Gail's friend."

"Yes, that is . . . I mean, I'm calling because it's very important to me that I talk to you." I heard a loud noise in my ears. It was my heart thumping. I wondered if the fat lady outside heard it, too.

There was a pause and then her voice came back on, sounding somewhat amused. "It seems to me that that might be a simple thing to arrange. What did you have in mind?"

I tried to read something into her words. "Could we meet for cocktails when you're through at work?"

She thought about it. "I have a dinner date at seven-thirty, but I guess, if we keep that in mind . . ."

"What time are you free?" The fat lady bumped her shopping bag against the door, on purpose or not, I couldn't tell and didn't care.

"Five-thirty? Would that be all right? The Darbury Room is right near here."

She could have said twelve midnight or twelve noon and I would have gotten there somehow. "I'll be there. And thanks a lot."

The amusement was very evident in her voice as she said, "No trouble at all. See you then." I stood there bemused after she'd hung up for at least a full minute and then finally replaced the receiver. The fat lady brushed by me as I came out of the booth. I ignored her. I couldn't get over how easy it had been. She must have felt the same magic. What a beautiful day it was, what a glorious day. I wanted to smile at everybody. I even felt like going back and apologizing to the fat lady. I let a car cut in front of me on the way back to division. What had I been worrying about an ugly world for? It was a sunlit, blue-skied, sparkling world.

Until Captain Granger told me to pick up Gail at La Femme at six. "She's got an idea. She called in on her lunch hour, but she didn't want to give it over the phone and besides, she says it's something for you. She said for you to wait down the street, where you were the other day. She doesn't want somebody at La Femme to spot you."

"Six," I said.

"Six," he repeated. I didn't dare look at him. "You got something else on your mind?"

I shook my head helplessly. "No. Six."

"And don't forget the funeral tomorrow."

"I won't." Six. How was I going to meet Pat at five-thirty and Gail at six? And I couldn't even get Benedict to sub for me, not the way Gail had put it to Granger. Damnation! Some days it didn't pay to get up.

10

I stood blinking in the entrance of the Darbury Room trying to adjust my eyes. It was pretty well filled, office
workers and such having a quick one after the day's toils.
I didn't see her right off and I thought maybe she hadn't
come. Maybe she was going to be late and I couldn't wait
too long. What would she think if she came and I wasn't
there? Dare I leave a message with the bartender? Did
he know her? Did she come in here a lot? Did she come
in here with Joe Harvard and those other guys, what were
their names, Terry and Leo? And were there others?
From her office? Standing room only, Gail had said. What
if we missed each other?

Then I saw her. Way over in the corner, smiling at me,
signaling with a slight gesture. I hurried across the room,
seeing no one. "Hi." I sat down in the chair across from
her, bumping someone in another chair behind me.

"Sorry," I said without looking. She wore a sort of tangerine-colored coat. She looked unbelievable.

"Hi. You look a little out of breath. We don't have to hurry that much."

"I'm afraid we do." I motioned to a waiter going past with a tray. "I'm the one that's put us in a bind. I have to be somewhere at six."

"Oh, dear. Then maybe you'd like us to have our talk another time. Although I think I can guess what it's about."

"You can?" I stared at her. She had felt it. The waiter appeared at my elbow just then. "What will you have?"

"Dubonnet on the rocks, please." I ordered it for her and a Heinekins for me. That noisy heart was at work again. I tried to calm it down by taking a long breath.

"Then we can skip the preliminaries," I said.

She smiled. "I think so."

I smiled back. It was the greatest, just to look at her. Her eyes were a kind of bluish purple. Her hair was maybe more silver than gold.

"The thing is," she said, "why don't you just tell Gail yourself?"

"I would have. Last night. Only I wasn't sure that the feeling was mutual."

"I don't think you need worry about that."

"That's a relief. Boy, is that a relief!"

"Well, now that you know, why don't you just go ahead? What do you want me to do?"

My answer was gleeful. "Just keep on doing what you are doing." The waiter showed up with the drinks.

"It's a little sad, really. Just when I thought I'd found myself the perfect roommate."

Nothing she could have said would have made me happier. I had never met a girl before who got the point even as you thought it, a girl who seemed to read my mind by intuition. Yes, I intended to marry her and the sooner the better. I wasn't getting any younger and I wanted to have children. I wondered how old she was and knew it didn't matter. She was younger than I and she would have beautiful children.

"Maybe the perfect female roommate." I grinned.

She blushed faintly. She sipped at her drink. I thought of her all done up in a fluffy pink robe across the breakfast table. I thought of her in a pure white nightgown and pushed that thought away. Looking to replace it, I remembered the theater tickets and I reached into my pocket for them.

She said, "Seriously, I'm very happy for you both."

My words came out too loud. "Who—both?"

She put her glass down, frowned an elegant little frown. "Why, you and Gail."

"Gail?" I yelped.

"Isn't that what you're talking about. You're going to ask Gail to marry you? You wanted to know if I thought she'd accept you? Isn't that what this is all about?"

"My God, no."

We looked at each other and her face began to color, slowly from the sweet curving lines of her throat up to her fine forehead. My hand, of its own volition, brought the tickets out of my pocket and held them up.

"I got these for tomorrow night," I all but whispered. "Will you come?"

She licked her lips with the tip of a slender pink tongue. She wanted to look down, I could tell, but I wouldn't let her.

After a while she said, "I can't. I've promised to go to the ballet and to dinner. . . ."

"Please."

"But I don't even . . . you're a friend of . . . I can't."

"You don't really know me, I know that. I want you to know me. I want to know you. How can we ever know each other if you won't go out with me? Yes, I'm Gail's friend, but that's all, her friend. I'm not in love with her, never have been. I went out and got these tickets to *Keep It in the Family* because I thought you liked the theater. I got them just for you. Please."

She glanced around as though people were listening. I didn't know or care if they were. She shook her shining head. "I can't." She closed her lips tightly.

"But why? Don't you like me?"

Her lashes fell against her cheekbones. When she raised them, her eyes were darker and quite cool. "I think you're a nice-looking, pleasant man. A stranger. I can't go with you tomorrow night because I have another engagement, an engagement with a man who has been a kind friend and I wouldn't do that to him. And now, if you'll permit me to remind you, it's nearly six and I think you'll be late for your appointment."

Involuntarily, I looked at my watch. It was five minutes of and I hadn't even paid the check. But how could I leave her like this? How could I?

I fished wildly for bills in my pocket, put three of them on the table. "But I can't use the tickets without you. I got them just for you." I put my hand across the table on hers.

She drew her hand away, put it in her lap. "I gather that this is an unusual reaction to your charms, Mr. Severson, and I'm sorry that you took so much for granted." I stood up, trying to say something, but she went on. "In the first place, I'm busy tomorrow night as I told you and in the second place, I saw *Keep It in the Family* last night."

Gail was pacing up and down the sidewalk when I reached the rendezvous. "Hurry up and get out of here," she said, sliding into the car as soon as I'd stopped. "I don't want anybody to spot you. It would spoil the whole thing."

Obediently, I drove off. "Whew," she said, "I'm glad to get away from there. I've got so much to tell you, Knute, and the main thing is about this Val, Mr. Valentine, you know, I mentioned him last night if you remember. . . ."

I nodded.

"Pull in over on Beacon Street so you can look at me. You don't look like you're listening to a word I'm saying. There's a space, right up there."

I did as she told me.

"Now. In the first place, I'd say this thing could easily be set up from La Femme. They do a lot of wigs there, as well as hair-on-the head. When they do wigs, they take names and addresses for a wig card file. It's necessary for keeping track of the wigs, you see, or otherwise they'd give Mrs. Jones' blond wig to Mrs. Smith and give her blond wig to Mrs. Jones. See what I mean?"

I nodded.

"They keep card files on regular customers, too. That's how they know when Mrs. Smith had her last permanent and her last coloring job, what they used on her head, et cetera. As I said, the addresses are included. What could be simpler than to take a list off the card files, run out some evening and give them the once-over. If it looks promising, cultivate the old girl a little further. Get an idea of the kind of jewelry she has, where she keeps it, when she's going to be away. There was a dizzy female in there today that would be perfect for such a setup. She was a new customer, covered in diamonds from here to here and talking loudly about making a trip to Expo before it's over."

"Did anybody take any special notice of her remarks?"

"It talks! I don't know what's the matter with you, Knute. You act like you're in another world. I think somebody did seem interested, but it wasn't obvious. I wouldn't have noticed if I hadn't been watching. That's why I want you to go to this—oh, what was the name of that place, I've got it jotted down here—go to Takpo's out in Brookline tonight. That's where Val spends his time, they tell me. He's a little bit of a problem in the shop because often he has a hangover and his work shows it."

"Val. Is this the one who was paying the attention to the woman with diamonds?"

"Yes. Dante was doing her hair and Val was in the next cubicle, I was helping him, and he kept walking around to the side near Dante's booth so he could hear better, at least that's what I thought he was doing."

"Takpo's. I'll see what I can do, but . . . how will I know this guy?"

Gail giggled. "In the first place, he's got these huge, baby-blue eyes. Dark curly hair that grows almost over his collar. Wears the most mod clothes you ever saw, big wide belts and broad-striped shirts and wild-colored jackets. He's as thin as a rail and not very tall. Little bitty feet, for a man. And those boot-like loafers with pointy toes."

"Sounds like you could spot him anywhere."

"Like my father used to say, you couldn't miss him in a plate of hash. Knute, is anything the matter? You look so . . . washed out."

"I'm fine. I'd better run you home if I'm going to get fed and dressed and out to Takpo's tonight. You sure he's going to be there?"

"Margot says it's his home away from home. They all whisper about it. They love to gossip, all of them. I'd forgotten what the atmosphere of a beauty shop is like. It just breeds pettiness."

I watched for a break in the going-home traffic to swing out. "I guess I'd better try and find something way out in my wardrobe," I said while waiting.

She giggled again. "It would help. And listen, I think we should keep an eye on that Mrs. Mason with the diamonds. . . ."

"Mrs. Mason!"

"Yes, some crazy name . . . Kay-Kay Mason, I think

it was. She was waving those diamonds around like she wanted them to be stolen."

I swore under my breath. "I told her not to look too prosperous."

"You told her? You mean you sent her there? Good grief, so that's why she did it. I thought she was acting like a character out of the comics. I hope nobody else got suspicious."

There was a gap in traffic. I pulled out into it and took off. I wondered fleetingly if there was any chance that Pat might be standing in front of the apartment or even looking out the window. . . . I turned that channel off right away. Keep my mind on business, that was my motto.

But, of course, there was no one on the sidewalk on Revere Street nor was there anyone at the window. I let Gail out and asked, "What is this Val's last name?" I couldn't bring it to mind.

"Cesare. Val Cesare. And Knute . . ."

I waited.

"I think he's just a teensy, weensy bit queer so watch it."

I opened my mouth and shut it, drove off. I couldn't be sure but I got the impression that she thought the whole bit was a hell of a funny story. Like the joke about the female who was slightly pregnant.

Women!

Takpo's was a dark little cave of a place lit here and there from the ceiling by murky blue spots. I thought, and I'm supposed to find a guy I don't know, a guy with big blue eyes, a weirdo. Everybody looked weird in that light and as for telling the color of anyone's eyes, forget it. I groped my way to the bar and ordered a beer while I tried to accustom my eyes to the joint. There seemed to be a bunch of people down near the back, but up at the bar with me were only three or four solitary drinkers.

I sipped at my beer and gradually began to make out forms and faces. Either my boy Val was one of the crew in the back, or he hadn't showed. I walked down to the jukebox and put in a quarter, eyeing as I went the hilarious group in the corner. They appeared to be cut of the same cloth, middle-aged refugees from the afternoon's baseball game according to the rolled-up baseball programs on the table. I went back to my barstool and nursed my brew.

Some girl was singing some song about Billy Joe jumping off the Tallahatchie bridge. I'd pushed the plungers on the jukebox at random and this, apparently, had been one of my choices. I got caught up in the lyrics, bemused by what the hell it had been they'd thrown off the bridge before Billy Joe had jumped, so that I didn't even notice the guy when he did come in.

He squatted on a stool round the corner from me, not too close and not too far away, I had the crawly feeling that he'd planned it that way in the same manner that a man takes a seat near a woman at a bar, provided that the woman is reasonably decent-looking, and ordered a scotch and soda in a dreamy voice. It was the voice that actually brought me out of my reverie and I looked over to see the biggest, roundest eyes I'd ever viewed on a man. There are prints in cheap art shops that remind me

125

of Val Cesare, kids with huge dark eyes, melting eyes begging for compassion. His eyes looked black like that in the kooky light of Takpo's and I had the weirdest feeling that they had a life of their own, those eyes, could move off that face and come over and sit on my cheek like dusty moths. I gave him a friendly look and ordered another beer. To the bartender I said, "Nice little place you've got here. This is the first time I've been in."

He looked back at me as though I was off my rocker, but then decided to humor me. "It's okay. Good neighborhood bar."

"Jerry's just sour on the world," spoke up Val Cesare. That voice sounded like syrup. "This is a good spot. A decent, friendly bunch." He raised his brand-new drink. "Welcome to the nest."

"Skol," I answered.

The jukebox sang out again. "On the South side of Chicago . . ."

"Pure corn," said Val. "Why don't you get some real music on that box, Jerry? The Lovin' Spoonfuls or the Jefferson Airplanes? Or even some of the new Beatle numbers?"

"I could care less what's on it," countered Jerry. "Me, I hate music. Any kind of music."

"You hear that? Can you conceive of a man who hates music?" Val shook his head in exaggerated wonderment and his long hair moved along his shirt collar.

Jerry gave him an acid stare and moved down the bar to answer another call for service. "I like to rag him," Val confided to me. Somehow he'd moved one barstool over. "It gets him wild."

126

The boys in the back room exploded into wild laughter and a waitress showed up, from nowhere as far as I could tell, I hadn't noticed her before, and gave Jerry a multiple order, apparently theirs. She was an incredibly thin girl with a flat chest, wearing a miniskirt that was mini-mini. "See Twiggy?" asked Val at my elbow. "Only the face isn't so famous. Hey, Jer, how about a refill?"

"Me, too, while you're at it, Jerry," I put my oar in. No sense in sitting there thirsty. Truth is, I was damn sure I couldn't sit there sober.

"You live around here?" asked Val.

I nodded, took a big swallow of beer, waved my hand vaguely.

"Me, too. I work in Boston, but I dig the suburbs. Better class of people out this way. Not so much riffraff."

"Uhmmm."

"Have a cigarette? These are Turkish. Nice for a change."

"No, thanks. I don't smoke. Used to, but I cut it out."

"Really? Hey, that's something. I wish I could. I've tried but by the second or third day I get positively witchy. How'd you do it?"

"Ate a lot of candy."

He nodded wisely. "That's what happens. I don't want to put on weight. I think it's too bad when a guy gets thick around the middle, don't you? I mean, you owe it to yourself to keep yourself in shape. You don't look like you have any trouble that way."

I finished the beer and ordered another. "Not much."

"And beer. Now I like beer, but it fills me up, you know.

You must drink a lot of it, but it doesn't seem to show on you."

"I'm lucky."

"I'd say so. Say, my name is Val Cesare. Might as well introduce ourselves."

I shook his hand. "Knute Severson."

"What do you do for a living, Knute?"

"I'm in insurance. Claims."

"Oh, yeah. They must keep you busy with all these crazy drivers. I won't have a car. Too much responsibility. Any place I want to go, I take a taxi. I got into that habit in New York. I worked there for several years, on Fifth Avenue. I'm a hair stylist. You know, fancy dos for rich, old women."

"Is that so? I've got a friend who's a barber."

He made a nothing gesture. "That's paupersville. Hairdressing, that's where the money is. Hey, Jerry, fill 'er up again and how about another beer for my friend, Knute, here? Sure you don't want something stronger?"

"No, thanks. If you get this one, I get the next one."

He smiled and his teeth glistened in the blue light. "Fair enough. Glad I ran into you tonight, Knute. I was feeling kind of down. A fellow alone can get to feeling that way. You married?"

I shook my head. "I was engaged once. She married the other fella."

He nodded again, sympathetically. "They'll do that. Women. You get to know them in my business. You'd be surprised at the stories I could tell you. Why, I've even had them make passes at me in the shampoo booth, can you imagine it?"

128

"Is that so?"

"Yeah, they're predatory, all right. Nothing surprises me any more. 'Course I was clued in before I ever got into hairdressing. I mean, my mother was a lulu." He laughed, a high, thin laugh. "But you don't want to hear the story of my life. What do you think about the Red Sox? Think they're going to take the pennant?"

"I sure hope so." I was getting a wow of a headache. If I'd had Gail Gregg handy, I would cheerfully have wrung her neck. Only it wasn't really her fault. It was a contact that had to be made. And I was the boy who had to make it. The beer tasted sour in my mouth.

"Say, Knute, what time is it? My watch is in the shop." He touched my arm, trying to read my wristwatch in the semi-darkness and it was all I could do not to pull away.

"Close to nine-thirty."

"Yeah? That's pretty early. Say, that gives me an idea. A friend of mine is having a blast. He invited me, but I told him I wasn't in the mood. Want to make the scene and see what's cooking? He collects some real kooks, you might get a charge out of them."

"Well, I don't know. . . ." This was exactly what I was looking for (and dreading), but I couldn't appear too eager. "I have to work tomorrow."

"Oh, what the hell. A man can live and die just sleeping and working. We owe it to ourselves to have a little fun, don't we? Come on, we'll get a taxi and hightail it over there. It isn't very far." He began gathering his cigarettes and lighter, his change from the bar.

"Well . . . okay, but I got a kind of headache coming on. Let me see if Jerry here has got an aspirin or something."

"That's too bad. Sure, he'll give you an aspirin, won't you, Jerry, old pal, old pal?"

The sour-looking bartender scowled. "Got to get it back in the office."

"Well, get it, man, get it. Me and Knute, we're going to blow this place." Val put his little face close to Jerry's. "You hear that, my friend and I are going to blow this crummy place."

"I don't like to leave the bar."

"Hah, you old bastard. I'll tend the bar for you, how's that? Little old Val will tend the bar." I realized that he was getting loaded. That was a break. I said, "Never mind, Jerry, I'll make out."

Jerry sighed. "Come on. Make it quick." And he ducked out the side of the bar and moved swiftly toward the back room. "Bartender, oh, bartender," caroled one of the drunks at the back table.

"Watch things a minute, Sally," he told the waitress, and we went into a small, cluttered room with a desk. There was a cabinet above the desk where he rummaged and produced an aspirin bottle. He doled a couple of the white tablets out to me. "Listen, bud. I'm a guy who keeps his mouth shut, but you know about that jerk you've taken up with, don't you? A word to the wise, like they say, is sufficient."

I played it the way I thought I should. I wouldn't meet his eyes. "I don't know what you're talking about."

"You don't, huh?" He looked at me a long minute, then, "You never can tell by looking," and he went out.

I followed him, popped the aspirin into my mouth, and chased them with the last swallow of beer in my glass. Val was standing by the bar, weaving slightly. "Are you ready, Knute?"

"I'm ready. No taxi though. My car's out front."

"Then we're off!"

The blast was being held in the basement apartment of a big, old brown Victorian house just off the Fenway. The place was wall-to-wall with people and they looked a little like cardboard figures on a billboard. I decided this was because the walls of each room had been painted in different poster colors, one color for each wall. One room was red, orange, blue, and white; another was purple, green, yellow, and pink. Between the visual effect and the noise, I would have gotten a headache, if I hadn't had a beaut to begin with. There was a guy sitting in a corner playing a wild-looking instrument that Val told me was a sitar. Its off-key twang pounded in my eardrums like background music for a madhouse. I discovered that there were boys and girls and men and women among the guests, but at first glance it was a little hard to tell. I stuck out like a sore thumb in my conventional jacket and slacks, shirt and tie. Furthermore, I'd had a haircut.

I never did discover who our host was. Val knew a good many people and I did my damnedest to remember their names, but the going was rough and I sure as hell couldn't whip out my notebook and jot them down. There wasn't any beer and I knew better than to go on liquor, so I tried to make do with wine. It was so sweet it was sickening. Val was bolting down anything he could get his hands on; I gathered the host's finances didn't include offering his guests scotch. He got drunker than he had been when we arrived, but once he reached a certain point, he just seemed to hang there. I was working like a mathematical genius to figure out a natural way to introduce the subject of larceny in one form or another, but I couldn't find an opening. It's not the easiest thing in the world to bring up as a topic of conversation, not even in those circles. Besides, the more I saw of Mr. Cesare, the more I was beginning to wonder if he could possibly be a part of a band of thieves. He was too untrustworthy, too vulnerable. How could they possibly trust him?

It was nearly midnight when I noticed the newcomer. He was a little taller than Val, a little heavier, and his dark hair was slicked down against his narrow head, was cut to a reasonable length, too. There was something Latin-looking about him, something that reminded me of something, and when I heard Val call him "Dante," I knew who he was. Another of the crew at La Femme, the one who Gail had said reminded her of a sheik. I knew, too, that he was furiously angry at Val.

"Dante, you old sweetheart!" Val threw his arms around him and swayed against him.

Dante coolly extricated himself. He was looking at me and I thought, oh, oh.

"Who's your friend?"

"My friend, Knute. My friend Knute, meet my friend Dante. Glad you could make it, old buddy. You've been neglecting your old pal Val."

I raised my jelly glass of wine in salutation. His eyes were cold black rocks. "Come on," he said to Val, "you're leaving."

"I'm not ready to go!" He set his small slim feet solidly, as solidly as he could, and glared at Dante. "You can't make me go. Knute won't let you." He made an imploring face at me.

Dante put a surprisingly large and strong-looking hand on Val's arm. The hand tightened and Val's face paled slightly. "No," he whimpered, and his huge eyes glistened.

"Maybe it is time that we went home." I moved forward with what I hoped was a foolishly amiable look on my face.

"I'll go with Knute. Not with you!" Val tried to pull away and got nowhere. His little feet made shuffling noises on the bare floor.

"Look, take it easy on him," I said. "He'll go."

"But not with you!" Val's voice was a squeak and, like a mouse, he slipped free and ran behind me. Dante stood tense. He was wearing casual pants and a turtlenecked sweater, dark in color. He looked like a Spanish flamenco dancer. He looked dangerous. What was this, a case of perverted jealousy, or was it something else?

A female in a floppy hat with ostrich feathers came staggering across the room and bumped Dante as she passed. None of us moved and I could hear snatches of conversation from behind me ". . . so I said how can you possibly believe a word that that McNamara says and he said . . ." and behind it all, that damn sitar.

"This is none of your business," said Dante quietly.

"Well, I know, but—" I couldn't come on too strong.

"He's drunk and he has to go to work tomorrow."

"He said he'd go."

From behind me, "With Knute. You'll hit me. I know the way you are."

"He won't hit you," I said. God, how sickening.

"I'm not going to do anything to him but take him home." Dante tried to smile, it was a tortuous attempt to wipe the fury off his face.

We stood in tableaux again and the pattern was broken by a line of people crawling across the floor on their hands and knees, coming between Val and me, crawling inexorably along for some unknown purpose, a line of traffic with no beginning and no end. They weren't making a sound, just crawling. The sitar played louder.

When I stood free of them, Dante and Val were gone. I set down the glass of wine on the nearest surface and looked for the front door. I couldn't remember whether the red, orange, blue, and white room came first or the purple, green, yellow, and pink room. I jerked open a door to a closet, slammed it shut, tried another; it was the entrance, all right, and under the clear night skies I could see two figures, one moving up and down over the other, at the curbside.

When I reached them, Val was whimpering and trying feebly to ward off the blows. That unexpectedly big hand at the end of Dante's slim arm was rhythmically pummeling him in the face and shoulders, the other hand holding him against my car. I went for Dante and pulled him backward. His body was muscled wire.

I tried to pin his arms but he seemed to have eight of them. Too late I remembered all the beer and the wine and too late I knew that I had underestimated him. I was hit by several sledgehammers and I went down.

11

"My God, Knute," said Benedict, "what happened to your eye?"

"Wow," said Pinkerton, "I'd say the lady had a boy-friend—or a husband."

"Shut up," I said to Pinkerton. To Benedict, I said, "Let's go see Granger."

We went in and I told the two of them the whole ignominious story.

Granger arranged his hands in steeple-shape. I thought, foolishly, of "here's the church and here's the steeple, open the doors and here's the people."

"Did he go through your pockets while you were out?"

"I think so. My wallet was shoved half-in, half-out my hip pocket when I came to. Of course, I'd taken out all my department stuff, the ID card, everything. Standard operating procedure."

137

"So you don't think they tumbled to the fact that you're police?"

"I don't see how."

"As far as I'm concerned," put in Benedict, "that rather cinches it. If that had been, I started to say an ordinary but I mean extraordinary lover's quarrel, I doubt if this Dante would have rifled your pockets."

"That's what I thought. But anybody looking on while we went at it would have figured it to be the trials and tribulations of a bunch of freaks. Or perhaps I should qualify that, anybody at that party would have thought so."

Granger got up. "You've done well, Knute. This Dante —what did you say his name actually is?"

"Julio Conti."

"This Julio Conti, we can begin bloodhounding him. Sooner or later, we'll get something to hang him up."

"He fits. I swear he fits. Personality, like a cobra. I think poor old Val got in on the deal and now they realize he's their weak spot. They should have known that to begin with. He's a drunk and a homo. Two chinks in his armor right off the bat."

Benedict said slowly, "He could be in danger."

I looked at him. "I've thought of that. But would they dare? It would bring the police to La Femme."

"Yes, they'll have considered that." Benedict's expression was troubled.

"Can we keep an eye on him?" I asked Granger.

He looked tentative. "I'd hate to get the wind up by putting tails on all of them. Still, I guess we'd better do

138

it—at least between their place of business and their homes."

"And there's something else." I told them about Kay-Kay Mason's tour de force the day before. "I'm going to call her off," I concluded, "but she may have triggered something."

"Martha and Mary! We can't guard the entire state. You'd better call the Wellesley police and tell them to keep a close eye on her place."

"Right. I'll get in touch with my friend Dennehy. He patrols out that way anyway."

"What are you going to do about that eye, Knute?" Now Granger looked paternal.

I grinned, or tried to. It hurt when the grin wrinkles came. "Wear dark glasses." I fished them out of my pocket and put them on. "There. How do I look?"

Benedict suppressed a smile. "Like Knute Severson with a black eye wearing dark glasses."

There was a knock then on Granger's door and Davoren looked in. "We're all set to leave for the funeral, Captain. You guys ready?"

"Moses on the mountain!" Granger looked at his watch. "I lost track of the time."

It was getting late. We almost fell over one another getting our coats and piling into the cars. A pair of meter maids were commissioned to answer the phones and I had a hunch that made Granger nervous, but every officer wanted to pay his respects to Cowan. "You come back as soon as it's over," he told Davoren just before he drove off with a carful. "Don't go to the cemetery. Just hightail it back to division."

139

"Yes, sir." We took off then, one car behind the other in a long line and passersby stopped to watch us drive away. We looked, I guess, like we were going somewhere important. We were.

The big Catholic church was filled. Almost every policeman in the city was there. Mary Cowan came down the aisle on the arm of her son. Both of them looked straight ahead, heads up. The casket was covered with hundreds, or so it seemed, of red roses, the flowers from the force. A single spray of white roses lay on top of that. Davoren whispered that the white roses were from the son and widow.

I sat there all through that mass trying not to hate the boy. His actions had caused this tragedy, but I tried to tell myself there were other reasons. A sound man doesn't suddenly crack when the pressure's put on. I kept telling myself that, not to do dishonor to Cowan, but to help Maurie. If I couldn't absolve him, how could he possibly absolve himself?

Mrs. Cowan didn't break down until the burial. I couldn't blame her. I don't usually go to interments, there's something about that box in the hole in the ground that strikes too close to home. Mrs. Casey and Casey rallied round her and the boy stood for a moment all alone while they comforted his mother.

His eyes were filled with unshed tears. His face was white and frightened. He looked very young, unfinished. I felt pity then and I might have been able to say something to him, something kind, but Benedict moved close to him and put his hand on Maurie's slumped shoulder. I turned away and, a few minutes later, we were all leav-

140

ing the sad scene. Nobody in our car said much during the ride back.

Among the messages waiting for us at Division Two was one from Gail Gregg. "She said she didn't think she could call back, she'd slipped out to telephone as it was," said the earnest-faced meter maid who'd taken the message. "She said to tell you Val hadn't showed up for work today and that you'd probably know about it, but if you didn't, you might want to know." She looked up at me. "Does that make sense to you?"

"Yes," I said briefly. "Come on, Benedict, let's get going."

Val Cesare's address was on the list I'd gotten from Agnew. The apartment house was new-looking, a brick complex on a side street in a good neighborhood. "Two-fifty a month?" I asked Benedict.

"Maybe more. I think you'd better go in alone if you still want to protect your cover."

"In case he's there, just nursing a hangover? Right. If he is there, I can fake it. Say I came to see how he is."

"Right. Let me know if you need me."

I left him sitting in the car while I went in and worked the self-service elevator. Val's apartment was on the fourth and top floor. I stepped out into a tiled hall and rang his doorbell. Rang it once, twice, three times with waits in between.

No answer.

I tried the doorknob. The door was locked. I turned around and took the elevator back downstairs. A sign reading Superintendent indicated a door at the rear of the first floor. I rang its doorbell.

A woman with her hair done up in pink plastic curlers opened it. "Yes?"

"I'm a friend of Val Cesare's," I told her, smiling politely. "I was just up there but he doesn't answer his bell and he isn't at work this morning so I'm afraid he may be ill. Could you possibly go in and make sure he's all right?"

She stared at me. I couldn't decide whether she was surprised that Val had a friend, or that I was his friend, or if she even knew who he was. "Well, I don't know . . ." she said at last. "My husband isn't here and we're not supposed to go into apartments for just any old reason."

"I assure you, I'm afraid something may be wrong."

"Why don't you call him on the telephone?"

"I did," I lied. "No answer."

"Then he's just probably away. Gone away somewhere. For the weekend."

"I was with him last night," I insisted. "He wasn't feeling well."

"All I can say is that if he was there, he'd answer the door or the phone. . . ." She was turning away.

"You wouldn't want me to go to the police, would you? I really am worried."

She stopped in her tracks. "Well, I never . . . wait till I get the keys, wait right there. What apartment is it?"

I told her. "Oh, top floor left," she said. "Now I remember him. Little fella with long hair and big eyes. Looks odd, but pays his rent. You wait here. Honestly, I don't know what this world is coming to, people can't mind their own business. . . ." Her voice trailed back

142

long after she'd disappeared from view, grew stronger as she came back into sight with keys in her hand. "All right, let's get this over with. I've got enough to do without chasing wild geese."

I stared at the ceiling as we went up in the elevator. I don't know what she looked at, but thankfully she was quiet. When we reached Val's door, she fumbled through her keys, thrust one in the lock, and turned it. The lock clicked and she opened the door.

"What in the world . . . ?" she said.

I came in behind her. The place was a mess, tables and chairs overturned, lamps on the floor, papers spilling out of and off of the desk, a shambles.

I walked swiftly past the woman and looked into the bedroom. Not so much mess there, but some, and no Val. The bathroom was prissy neat and empty. Ditto the kitchen.

"I don't know what's going on here," said the superintendent's lady when I came back into the living room, "but I'm calling the police."

"You won't need to," I told her, showing my ID card. "My partner's in a car downstairs in the parking lot. When you go down, would you mind asking him to come up?"

"Why in the world didn't you say so in the first place?" she grumbled. "I don't know what things are coming to, police who pretend they aren't police . . ." She disappeared into the hall and immediately after I heard the elevator departing.

I began to pick up the spilled papers, looking them over as I did so. There were cancelled checks and bank statements, might be something interesting there but it would take an accountant to make any sense out of them. I put in a quick call to Granger, asked for a working crew as soon as possible, and was just hanging up when Benedict came in. He whistled softly.

"I'm afraid we're too late," I said ruefully.

"Any sign of him?"

"No. If it goes according to Hoyle, he'll undoubtedly turn up in the harbor somewhere. Face down."

"If he turns up at all." He nudged a table lamp lying on the floor with his toe. "I wonder what they were looking for?"

"Could be anything. I wouldn't put it past a Val Cesare to keep a diary. In purple ink."

"Perhaps they didn't find whatever it was."

"They did. In the bedroom, I'd guess. They stopped the rampage in there. The rest of the place is as neat as a pin."

Benedict thrust his hands in his pockets, looked around. "Too bad. I have an odd feeling about this business."

"What do you mean?"

"It's too pat. Rings as though it were borrowed from a scenario. Everyone's playing his part to perfection. Take this, for example. It looks like a stage set."

"I know what you mean. I feel as though I'd stepped into a George Segal role. All this undercover stuff. Do you suppose somebody's tumbled?"

"I wonder."

I straightened a chair and sat down. "If they have, how? Gail Gregg? My little charade last night?"

Benedict took his hands out of his pockets and lit a cigarette. "God knows."

I thought about it. "It could go back to the Prescotts. But I don't see how."

"Unless the husband wanted her dead." He blew smoke and looked owlish.

I stood up. "Damn. As I see it, there's only one thing to do."

"And that is?"

"Play along with it. Go on with the whole production, just as we plotted it. But, at the same time, look further into Shaw Prescott's background and anyone else's we can connect with it in any way."

"The key to the thing is why. Robbery is done for profit, primarily. But it could also be motivated by the need for excitement, the thrill of beating the law. Take Teddy Green, the bank robber, for instance. It's obvious the man could have been a successful businessman, so why did he rob banks? Why did he choose a life of crime that resulted in his incarceration for the major part of his adult life? I'd say he enjoyed his chosen profession, wouldn't you?"

"Something like an inveterate gambler? All or nothing?"

"Something like that."

"If your theory is correct, almost any one might have a motive for crime. Draper Prescott, Shaw Prescott, even a woman." I looked at him. "Why not a woman?"

"Why not?"

"It's too devious. If I've learned anything, it's that

145

people behave in character. If they've flipped, they show it if you just know where to look."

"Ah. There's the rub. If you know where to look. Then, too, you assume they've flipped. I've seen more criminals who were coldly, calculatingly sane than I've ever seen madmen."

"Oh, I know. Legally sane. But I still think anybody who goes out of his way to live that dangerously is nuts."

"That's because you're a conservative man, Knute. Your behavior patterns are rigidly conformist. You never would have been a riverboat gambler. Nor a prospector for gold."

What he said nettled me. "I suppose that means I'm as dull as hell."

Benedict smiled soothingly. "No, that doesn't mean that at all. If you were a man who eschewed excitement and violence, you never would have chosen your present profession. You'd have gone into an office somewhere. I simply mean that your great difficulty is recognizing that strain of amorality that says 'I do as I please. I am above the law because the law is not for me.' You call it madness and I say it is a facet of human personality."

I shrugged. I couldn't hold my own with him in such a discussion and I wanted to drop it. I started in on the desk and after a few minutes, he went into the bedroom and poked around in there. We didn't disturb too much because of possible fingerprints and when the technical crew arrived, we left them to it. I almost expected to see Cowan with his camera, but there was a new guy named Gilbreath instead and that's the way life goes. Somebody's always around to take your place. I drove away from Val Cesare's apartment feeling downright sour.

Until I got back to division. I had a message that Pat Drake had called.

My fingers stumbled in dialing the number. I recognized her cool "Hello" instantly and I said, "This is Knute Severson. You called me?"

"Oh, yes." Her voice changed, became flustered. "I wanted to—that is, I think I owe you an apology. I mean, I know I owe you an apology."

I grinned at the telephone. "Think nothing of it. I've still got the tickets."

"I'm sorry, I still can't go tonight but I do want to apologize properly and explain . . . if you could drop by for a few minutes around five?"

"Sure. I'll be there." Would I ever be there! I hung up, silently singing. Gail wouldn't be there, she didn't get through at La Femme until six, which reminded me that I wanted to see her but not at five o'clock! We had planned to put a tail on Julio Conti when he left work and we'd decided to visit Shaw Prescott's mutual fund offices as soon as we could make contact, Monday, probably, they'd be closed Sunday.

I was almost at Pat's door before I remembered that I'd forgotten to call Dennehy in Wellesley about Kay-Kay Mason. I'd do it later, I promised myself, and found a parking place, hurried to get to where I was going.

It wasn't until she answered the door that I remembered my black eye. She reminded me, the way she looked at it. "It's nothing," I said. "Just a little fracas. You look great."

She did, oh, yes, she did. Pure and virginal in a white wool robe buttoned from high neck to full skirt. Her hair was tied back with a pale blue satin ribbon.

"Forgive me for not dressing. I'm going out at seven. I've mixed you a martini. I know you like them. Come in." She wouldn't meet my eyes after that first horrified glance at the condition of my face.

I repeated, "You look great." I didn't tell her I was more of a beer drinker than a martini drinker. That would come later and we'd laugh about it.

"Sit down, won't you?" She took my poplin raincoat. I loved to watch her going and coming. She brought me the cocktail glass like a Greek maiden with an offering. "Thanks," I said and sipped it. It was a little heavy on the vermouth.

"I was terribly gauche yesterday," she began when she'd seated herself in a chair, a rather faraway chair I noticed without pleasure. "I wanted to tell you face to face how sorry I am. I talked to Gail, you see, and it seems I assumed a great deal that wasn't so."

"I told you. We're friends. That's all."

She nodded solemnly. "That's what Gail said. I was terribly troubled. I don't like women who, who poach on another's property. I don't like to be in that position, even inadvertently."

"You're not." I inched forward in my chair. It was the only way I could get closer to her at the moment.

"But then, that left me in another situation that I found distasteful." She definitely was avoiding looking at me now.

"You mean you don't want any part of me?" I laid it on the line.

She gave me a swift, startled glance. "It isn't that. I don't know if Gail told you, I'm a widow. I don't date, not in the regular sense." She moved her hands nervously in her lap.

"Then, who is Tom, Dick, and Harry? I mean, those three guys you run around with?" There was a hard edge to my voice but I didn't give a damn. I didn't like runarounds.

"That's just it. They're friends of Win, my husband. They were in the service with him, they share my feelings about—what happened. They treat me in a special way." She laced her fingers. "It's a bit hard to explain."

"You mean like the princess in the tower? The Lily Maid of Astolat?"

"Something like that." She looked humble. "I don't know what I'd do without them. I think I'd go mad."

"They gravitate around the Queen Bee, seeing that she's properly entertained, is that it?" I put the still full martini glass on the nearest table.

"It sounds horrible the way you say it!" She stood up and moved toward the window. "It isn't. It isn't at all. It's lovely."

"I'll bet it is. What do you do when you're out, talk about the late-lamented? I think Gail told me he died over a year ago."

Her look was supposed to be putting me in my place. "One year, two weeks, and three days. Yes, of course. We do speak of him. Often."

I got up, too. "Well, good luck to you. May you enjoy

your little string quartet forever. My coat's in the closet, isn't it?"

"You don't understand!" With her hands clasped, she looked like an angel on a candy box.

"I understand, all right. Because I happen to find you attractive as a woman and not as an extenuation of a dead man, I can't play in your park. Isn't that it?"

"I thought, if you understood how it was, how I can't . . . I thought if you understood, maybe we could see one another occasionally."

"You mean, if I'll behave myself you'll fit me into your ring-around-a-rosy? Thanks, but no thanks." I jerked open the closet door, grabbed my coat.

There were red spots in her pale cheeks. "Then I've wasted our time, haven't I?"

"I don't know about yours, sweetie, but you've certainly wasted mine. I don't dig marble statues."

"And I don't dig, as you put it so elegantly, animal-men!"

I never hit a woman in my life, but so help me, I felt like it then. "Look here," I told her, just barely getting control of myself, "I'm a pretty ordinary guy with ordinary tendencies. In my world, when an ordinary guy falls in love with a woman, he wants to sometimes hold her hand, kiss her, ordinary things like that. He wants her to look at him and see him, to talk to him about him. If there are restrictions on their relationship, he wants them to be mutually decided restrictions, not dictated sets of rules. He wants things to be right and normal, sometimes beautiful and sometimes maybe even dull, the way life is. I'll grant you it was pretty stupid of me to fall in

150

love with the way you look without waiting to find out
the way you were inside. But I did, and that's the reason
I made this damn fool of myself six ways from Sunday.
So if that makes me an animal, then that's what I am.
You just forgive and forget it, and say that's the way of
the beast because you come from a quite different spe-
cies, if you want my opinion. You may be as fair as the
angels, but to me you're the black widow spider." And
I turned on my heel and walked out.

I guess I told her. Sure I did.

She was sick, that's what she was. Living in the past
with a ghost. I couldn't get mixed up in such a situation,
I couldn't. And yet I almost was . . . no, that wasn't
true either, I was still. Because she attracted me in a
way no other woman had ever attracted me. Hell's bells,
it was impossible. All my instincts told me to run, man,
run in the opposite direction. And that's what I was
doing.

I thrust the envelope with the theater tickets in a litter
basket on the way to the car. Pure waste, but I didn't
even want to look at them. It was nearly six o'clock, I
wondered if I'd be able to catch Gail at La Femme. I
wanted to know the scoop on Val Cesare and then, too,
I could give her my succinct opinion of her charming
roommate. Should I do that? What business was it of
mine? Leave it, that's what I should do. Run. I took off
like a rocket and zigged and zagged my way back to
Newbury Street. Just as I was passing the beauty shop,
the Spanish door opened and Gail came out accompanied
by another female. I drove on past, up to the next block,

and waited double parked, no parking space being available, naturally.

She was alone when she drew abreast of the car, but not looking my way, and I gave her a small beep. She looked behind her before she came over and got in. "Did Val show up?" I asked her.

"No." She leaned back and closed her eyes. "I'm beat. We had a busy day and I'm out of practice."

"What was said about his no-show?"

"Margot was annoyed. She called his apartment and got no answer. That's when I slipped out and called you."

"Did any of the others say anything?"

"The others just looked bored. But after lunch, Dante took off, too."

I almost ran into the car ahead of me. "When?"

"He didn't come back from lunch, that's all I know. Besides, weren't you watching him?"

I swore under my breath. "The tail was supposed to pick him up at six. He's probably still standing back there, waiting for him." This was a fouled-up business, my whole life these days was fouled up. "I'm going back to division. Do you want to go there or get a taxi?"

"Taxi!" She sat up straight. "I'm the subway type, myself. Let me out at the Exeter Street corner, I'll walk back to Dartmouth."

I pulled up and let her out. "Sorry, Gail," I said. "This may be important."

"I know. Thanks anyway." She began to walk away. I didn't wait to see her go, but took off again. Back at the office, I found Granger out to supper and nobody around who could do me any good. I called Robbery, the powers that be were out there, too. Saturday night on the town, or some such. I left a message. They had more manpower than we did. But I didn't have much faith in the status quo. I decided to run by the Conti apartment myself. I had the address on Agnew's list.

Julio Conti alias Dante lived in the South End. With his sister and brother-in-law, I discovered when I found the right door and rang the right doorbell. The sister was beginning to go to seed, but she was all done up in a high hairdo and a cocktail dress. "Julio isn't home," she told me without expression. "He don't get off work till six o'clock. He don't get home till late sometimes."

"Sofia!" shouted a man's voice from the interior of the apartment, "Sofia, this kid needs something done to him. He's wet again."

"I'm coming," she called over her shoulder. "If you want to see Julio, best thing you can do is see him at La Femme on Monday. I don't know when he's in or out." The door began to close on me.

I flashed my ID. "Police."

The dark eyes narrowed. "I don't know nothing." The door continued to close. I stuck my foot and arm in it, pushed it open. I could see the room now, see a man come into it holding a baby, a boy bare from the waist down. "What's going on here?" asked the man.

"He wants Julio."

"He ain't here."

"I told him. He's a cop."

The look he gave her said, don't you think I know that?

"Has he got a friend, a Val Cesare?"

153

The man began to swear in Italian.

"That—fink." Julio's sister's mouth curled. "No wonder he's in trouble if it's got anything to do with that queen."

The baby began to wail.

"Look, we don't know nothing." The woman went to take the baby as she talked, took it from her husband and held it away from her so as not to soil her dress. "Shhh, shhh," she whispered to it.

"We're fixing to go out," said the man. He gestured toward the infant. "Soon as we get him down to Mrs. Petchelli's."

I hesitated. I didn't know how far to go. If I let on that I was the guy who'd been with Val last night, I'd blow the gaff. "I'm looking for Val Cesare, he's a missing person. He's disappeared from the beauty shop, didn't come in this morning, and then after lunch, your brother didn't come back. You got any idea where he could be?"

They looked at each other. "You tried the Kline woman's?" asked the man.

"Margot Kline's?"

"That's her."

"Thanks." I started for the door just as the woman said, "Hand me a diaper, will you? Don't just stand there." I closed the door on them, the woman pinning a new diaper on the baby on the sofa, but not looking at the baby; both she and her husband kept their dark eyes on my face and then, when it was gone, I guess they just kept watching the closed door. They were looking for some answer in that doorway, but I didn't have it. I only had the questions.

I had to go back to division to get Margot Kline's address. Traffic was tough and my temper was worse. I

remembered on the way that I had the black eye, that
Julio's sister and brother-in-law would tell him some cop
with a black eye was there looking for him and if he was
as smart as I thought he was, he'd put two and two together without a slide rule. We were going to lose these
pigeons as sure as shooting. I felt it in my bones and I
knew, too, that I was running around like a chicken without a head. I thought of calling Benedict, but decided
against it. I'd go by the Kline woman's, maybe Julio was
there. If I could just get my hands on him, maybe I could
save the day.

Margot Kline lived off Storrow Drive near the river.
That figured; she was Agnew's girl friend, he would set
her up some place nice. What was she doing entertaining
Julio Conti, if she was? Agnew had said he'd be out of
town, that was it. Cat's away and mice will play. I went
up in the elevator and sounded her doorbell. I should, I
reflected, go into the Fuller brush business.

Nobody answered.

I rang again, harder.

Still no answer.

I rang long and loud and waited. I couldn't hear a
sound.

I said to hell with it.

I stood there. There wasn't any place to wait, just
the hall, bare except for a brown carpet and a fake plant.

I got in the elevator and rode down. I stood on the
sidewalk and waited some more, but nobody came who
looked like a Margot Kline.

At last, for some reason I'll never know clearly, I
drove back to division instead of going home.

12

One of the night boys was kind enough to bring me back a sandwich and coffee and I spent my time going over a list of possibles. Possible whats, I wasn't sure. I sat and scribbled down the names of everyone I could think of who'd had any pertinent contact with Dorinda Prescott. I felt like Hercules Poirot, but what else did I have to do with my time?

Mr. and Mrs. Draper Prescott. No police record whatsoever, not even a traffic violation. In Europe, or en route home, at the time of the burglary. No known motive for burglarizing their own home—insurance? Doubtful, but check finances. (Was the safe open or was the combination known to the thieves?)

Shaw Prescott. Arrested in 1962 for driving through a red light, lost license for seven days. In the Virgin Islands at the time of the burglary and murder, verified

157

by cable from authorities there. Only possible motive—elimination of wife, set up to look like burglary. Question—would either Draper or Shaw be able to make contact with criminals to pull off caper? Good question. Not likely, but anything's possible. Suggestion of philandering. Was there another woman? No evidence of other woman. Further investigation needed.

Mr. and Mrs. Gregory Hinchliffe. Hardly worth considering, but I put their names down anyway. Motives? None known. Repeat, hardly worth considering.

Kay-Kay Mason. Arrested for disturbing the peace in 1965, complainant was husband; arrested drunken driving same year, lost license for three months. Possible motive? She lives right next door. Even though she's older, she's attractive. Could she possibly have been the other woman in Shaw Prescott's life? Doubtful, but not impossible. Incidental intelligence, full name Katherine Karen Mason.

Herman Agnew. No police record. Big name in finance, construction, politics, etc. Philanthropist, known for charity efforts in behalf of crippled children, mental hospitals, unwed mothers. Came up the hard way, Roxbury boy. Hard as nails but considered fair. Only connection, he owns La Femme. Question—is La Femme some sort of red herring I dreamed up?

Impossible. If so, explain Val Cesare and Julio Conti.

All right, explain. Val and Julio are a duo. Val, playing the feminine part, has wandering eye. Julio jealous. Nothing more, nothing less.

I don't buy it. Can't say positively why, but they smell to high heaven. Or maybe I'm hoist on my own petard.

I dreamed up La Femme connection. Maybe I'm stuck with it.

All right, back to the beginning. If it was just an out and out burglary with no funny business, how come all three women robbed that weekend were La Femme customers? That reminded me that Robbery was supposed to be taking my theory a few steps further. I called them for the second time that night and patiently explained what I wanted. "Lieutenant Burbank's out on prowl," said the voice on the other end. "He'll have to call you back. I don't know anything about it."

Frustrated again, I went back to my pencil work. Because we'd approached this thing obliquely, we had no idea whether Val and Julio-Dante had any alibis for the times in question or not. I made a neat list of probable hours and dates of the burglaries, put it in my wallet for future use. Even if we picked them up that very night, caught in the act, nailing them was going to be a long, involved procedure.

Were there just the two of them? Could be. None of the witnesses had spotted more than two, but . . . I went through my notes again. I'd checked the records on the other male employees at La Femme. Minor traffic violations for John Keith, Robert Ogden, and Harold Finch, nothing for Joseph Grebe, an assault and battery for Julio, that figured, and a sexual offense for Val. That figured, too.

The male employees. That brought me back to the heretofore unseen Margot Kline. What was it Agnew had said about her? Ambitious, no, that wasn't the word. Greedy. I wondered if she was home yet. Idly, I dialed her phone number, let it ring a dozen times. No soap. Back to my squirrel in the cage routine.

Granger came in about ten. "Don't you ever stay home?" I asked him jokingly. He could be found at division at all hours, I knew that. He'd miss it if he retired, he'd made his job his life.

"What are you doing here?" he countered.

I indicated the scribbled sheets of paper. "Trying to make some sense out of this thing. It's driving me bananas."

He started to say something, but before he got the words out of his mouth, my phone rang. I said, "That'll be Burbank from Robbery," and picked it up. A somewhat familiar voice said, "Severson? Is this Detective Severson? I didn't know whether you'd be on duty or not, but I thought I'd better take a chance."

"Who's this?"

"Dennehy. Out in Wellesley. You told me to call you if anything came up. . . ."

"What's happened? What's come up?"

"I think it's this gang you were looking for. They broke into this Mrs. Mason's house and they really worked her over. . . ."

"Kay-Kay Mason? Is she all right?"

"Well, I wouldn't call her all right, exactly. We took her to the Newton-Wellesley Hospital."

"Where are you now?"

"At her house."

"I'll be out as soon as I can get there." Granger made motions and I added, "Ask your chief if it's okay with him."

"I already asked him. He said he didn't care who came in, as long as we get these guys. He doesn't go for this kind of business in our town."

"I'll be right along. You wait for me." I hung up and stuffed my paper work in my coat pocket. "I don't know what it means," I told Granger, "but they took the bait. Too well. And too quick. That's what I don't like about it."

"I think I'll come along with you." Granger fell in step.

"Sure." I didn't know whether I liked that or not. I'd never worked with Granger, but he was coming and that was that. I wished it were Benedict. Benedict had a sixth sense or something. Hadn't he said, "It's too pat?"

We got to Wellesley in twenty minutes by my watch. There were two police cars in Kay-Kay Mason's drive and a uniformed officer was guarding the door. We told him who we were and he said Chief Grace was expecting us, so we went in. I had to step over something in the hall, a clump of something, like a lost dust mop, and I peered at it, realized it was the dog, Pujums. Quite dead, its little body limp and bloody. "I think they kicked it to death," said Dennehy, who came to meet us.

Kay-Kay's modern living room looked worse than Val's place had. "It looks like pure wanton destruction as much as anything else," Chief Grace told us after we'd all been properly introduced.

"It's possible," I agreed. No one knew better than I that it was possible. I'd forgotten Kay-Kay; I'd gotten her involved in this and they knew it, whoever they were, and they'd come to show me that they knew, knew all about it. Thumbing their noses at me. They must have

161

had my number from the time I'd hooked up with Val. Julio's appearance was no accident then. But, how? Gail had been the one to set Val up, surely not Gail . . . surely not. I knew better than that. Who else could have known? Someone saw her with me? Could be. But that still didn't explain how they knew who I was.

I came out of my reverie to hear Chief Grace say, "We took her in the police ambulance. She was badly beaten, but conscious. I don't think she was coherent, though. She said something about being useful was for the birds."

"Did they get anything? Jewelry, anything else?"

"I guess they got her jewelry, all right. We found an empty jewelry box and she mumbled something about diamonds weren't a girl's best friend. I think she was out of her head."

"She was making a funny," I told Chief Grace. "That's the way she is. I'd like to go over to the hospital, Captain, if it's all right with you."

"You'll send us a report?" Granger asked Grace.

"Why not? We'll take all the help we can get. We have enough problems as it is."

They shook hands and Dennehy took me aside to say, "Hey, remember I told you I'd seen that guy Prescott somewhere?"

I nodded.

"Well, I figured it out. I was just over there to see if he'd heard anything; he hadn't, and I got a good look at him. You know where I'd seen him? In the movies! He looks just like that guy Alfie, Michael Caine."

I controlled myself. "Yeah, see what you mean. You say

he didn't hear anything? He couldn't possibly have had any part in this, could he?"

Dennehy's eyes grew round. "Jeez, no. I mean, I'm sure not. He was kind of otherwise occupied, you know what I mean?"

"No. What do you mean?"

"Well, with a woman. I got the impression they'd been necking up a storm. They were dressed and all that, but . . . well, you can tell. They looked kind of blind-eyed."

"Who was she?"

"Some airline stewardess. I've got her name here." He read it to me from his notebook. I'd never heard it before, but I could have bet my bottom dollar she made the Virgin Island run.

"Ready, Knute? Chief Grace will fill us in tomorrow." Granger was at my elbow.

"Fine. Let's go. Thanks for the cooperation, Dennehy, Chief Grace." I nodded to the other officers and we took off for the Newton-Wellesley.

A Dr. Torrence was tending Kay-Kay and he'd just given her something to knock her out. "She's going to be all right," he told us, "but she won't look too pretty for a few days. Were you in on the same fracas, Detective Severson?"

I touched my black eye. I kept forgetting it. "Sort of. We'd like very much to see her. Do you think she's asleep yet?"

"We can see, but she needs rest."

"We won't be long. It's important."

He took us in and I thought she'd gone by-by but she

opened her eyes when she heard us and said, "Where were you when the lights went out?"

"I'm sorry, Kay-Kay. Damn sorry." She looked a mess. They'd cleaned her up, but her face was a mass of bruises and her eyes and lips were swollen.

"I think they killed Pujums. He was an awful nuisance, but they didn't need to do that." Her eyelids were heavy, they drooped.

"It's all my fault," I told her, "and I don't know how to make up for it. I meant to call the local police and alert them, but I got involved in something else and I just plain forgot. It's all my fault"—I took her hand and patted it—"the whole thing."

She tried to smile. "You're a sweet boy, but I didn't follow orders, did I? You told me not to look too prosperous, but I went in there like Mrs. Gotrocks. It's my own damn fault. I tried for a grand slam and I got one, too!" That remark amused her and her eyelids drooped again.

"Kay-Kay, we're going to go. I'll see you tomorrow, but there's just one thing, one thing I've got to know. Did you recognize any of them? Had you seen them at La Femme? Kay-Kay, do you hear me? I've got to know."

She tried to open her eyes, but couldn't. Her lips moved drowsily. "I never saw any one of them, there were three, I never saw them in my whole life, I . . . never . . ." She was gone to dreamland. As for me, I was gone, too. All gone. Down and out.

It took us thirty minutes to get back to division and I spent that time trying to explain to Granger. I told him Benedict's hunch about the patness of the whole thing and I reviewed the paper work I'd struggled with earlier.

He listened without comment and, as I parked the car, I summed up. "So it seems that I've goofed but good. To tell you the truth, I don't know which way to jump."

Granger opened his door, put one foot out. "I'm not trying to play the old professor, Knute, but I think you've got your finger on it. If I were you, there's one person that you mentioned that I'd try to talk to right away. You think about it and if it doesn't come to you, I'll spell it out. 'Course I could be wrong, too, I'm not as close to the case as you are. But it seems to me that all hades started breaking loose right after you met up with one fella."

I stared at him openmouthed. He put the other foot out and stood up. "I think I'll hit the hay, Knute. I'll see you in the morning."

"Captain Granger," I called after him, "I've thought of that, but it can't be. How could it be?"

He stopped. I could see the middle of him through the car window, kind of paunchy. "You're in a business," he said, "where anything's possible."

I heard him walk away then, heard him faintly because there were loud noises, conversations going on in my head. I'd started at the wrong end. The cart before the horse. The evidence was there all the time, but we'd tried to work it from the wrong angle. They couldn't have gotten rid of the evidence, could they have? Gail would have noticed at once. Too many other people would have noticed and wondered. They didn't dare and besides that, there was an arrogance in everything they did that said "To hell with the cops!"

And the word that made the loudest noise and was said the most often in my head was, "Why? But why?"

Benedict and I went to Margot Kline's early Sunday morning, as early as we could since it took me a few minutes to bring him up to date.

"Do you think Julio will be there?" he wanted to know.

"It would be a plus if he is, but nothing has worked right so far, so I doubt it." I hadn't had much sleep and I didn't feel very hopeful. Too many things could go wrong. Time, that's what this mess was going to take, a lot of luck and time. The best we could hope for right off was that we could scare them off the housebreaks. Maybe that would have to be enough. You take what you can get.

Margot Kline's apartment house was quiet in the early morning sunshine. "I've never seen finer September weather," commented Benedict as we crossed the parking lot.

I squinted up at the sky. "Nary a cloud."

I rang the Kline woman's doorbell with authority. If she wasn't there this time, I was armed with a search warrant for her place and for La Femme, too. "We were damn fools that we didn't come here in the first place," I told Benedict while we waited. "She runs La Femme. She was the obvious one."

"He steered you off her rather neatly," agreed Benedict. We heard faint sounds inside the apartment. I rang again.

Footsteps approached, slowly and from some distance away. A sleepy feminine voice said, "Just a minute. Hold your horses. Who are you? What do you want?"

This last was said through a slit in the door as a pair of dark eyes looked out at us over a chain.

"Margot Kline? We're the police. We'd like to talk to you, please." I held up my ID card.

The eyes grew brighter. "The police? But, what . . . just a minute, I can't get this darn chain undone . . . there. Now what in the world do you want with me?"

She was a big girl and when Gail had suggested she was beautifully built, she wasn't kidding. Her hair was long and auburn, hanging down her back and shoulders. She wore a pink negligee, a little sheer for the purpose of greeting two detectives, and her feet were bare. Even her feet were sexy-looking. She backed into the room as we came in and her eyes looked frightened.

"Anybody here with you?" I asked.

She shook her head. "No. Of course not. I live alone."

"Where were you last night?"

"I was out. Out with friends. Why should you care where I was last night?"

"Have you seen Julio Conti lately?" I kept walking forward, she kept backing up. She ran into the side of an armchair and stopped.

Her eyes cleared. "Julio? So that's what it's about. No. He left work at lunchtime yesterday, he works for me, he's a hairdresser, and I haven't seen him since. Has anything happened to him?"

"What about Val Cesare?"

"No. Val didn't show up at all. Won't you sit down? Gosh, you scared me to death. What's happened to them? That's why you're here, isn't it? Because something's happened?"

I looked around the room. Draw drapes covered an entire wall that must look toward the river. I walked over and pulled them back. Sunlight flowed in. The carpet was pink and so were the walls. A symphony in soft, rosy pink. Greedy. That's what Herman Agnew had said. He should know.

"What makes you think something has happened to them?" I asked. "What do you think could have happened to them?"

"I don't know. I mean, they did just go off, or something, without a word. And they are sort of strange, I suppose you know all about that. . . ." She stopped. She thought she had it all figured out, but now she wasn't so sure.

While we'd been talking, Benedict had been looking in the other rooms. He came back now and made a negative movement with his head.

"All right, Miss Kline. Get dressed." My tone suggested she make it snappy.

"But why—where are you taking me?" She hugged the robe to her suddenly as though she had realized it was diaphanous.

"We're going down to your beauty shop to get your customer record files," I told her frankly. "Something we should have done in the beginning and we would have except we were afraid we'd scare them off."

"Scare them off?" She tried to smile. "You mean Val and Dante? What have they done?"

I ignored her questions. "And when we get those customer files, do you know what we're going to do with them? We're going to take them down to Division Two and check them against every unsolved housebreak in the greater Boston area in the past two years. That's how long you've been running La Femme, isn't it, Miss Kline?"

I thought for an instant that her hair had suddenly flamed, but then realized the illusion was caused by her face being so white.

"Housebreaks?" she said.

"Get dressed," I said.

She took a deep breath and her bosom moved and when it moved, it moved. "I don't know what you're talking about," she said coldly, "but it sounds to me as though I need a lawyer."

"Please call one," I said sweetly. "You have a right to remain silent. Anything you say can and will be used as evidence against you in court. You have a right to consult a lawyer of your own choice before you answer any questions, and to have that lawyer present while you answer any questions. If you are unable to hire a lawyer, a lawyer will be provided before you are asked any questions." I beamed at her.

"And, " Benedict added, "if you answer any questions, you have the right to stop anytime during the questioning that you wish to do so. Do you understand your rights?"

She flared. "Of course I do. What do you think I am, an idiot?" She paused, visibly softened. "You make this sound serious." She looked wistful and very feminine. Somehow the pink negligee had come partway open.

"Miss Kline," I said, "you can take my word for it. It is serious. Now be a good little girl and go get dressed."

13

Thirty-two of the names in the La Femme files had been hit by burglars in the two-year period that La Femme had been in business.

The Robbery Squad began its chore of investigating every past and present employee but it looked as though only Val Cesare and Julio Conti were active participants and both were still missing. And Margot Kline. Dear greedy Margot. There'd been one diamond necklace she'd been unable to part with.

We zeroed in on Margot. The lawyer she called showed up, but he was nervous. "I do Miss Kline's income tax," he told us. "I'm not an expert in these matters."

We asked her if she wanted to call someone else. She hesitated. I could read her mind. Her chum Herman Agnew had able lawyers. She was torn between involving him and saving her own skin.

"Mr. Agnew out of town?" I asked conversationally. Benedict, Granger, and Burbank from Robbery were all sitting in on our little meeting.

She looked innocent, as innocent as she could look. "How would I know?"

"You should. According to him, you two are more than friendly."

She flushed, tossed her head.

Denbeaux, her lawyer, spoke up. "Miss Kline, I must reiterate that I'm not qualified to give you adequate counsel. If you won't call another attorney, I can only tell you that you are not required to answer these questions. You have the right to remain silent."

I seconded him. "Yes, that's true. We told you that before. When we find Val Cesare and Julio Conti, and we will find them if they're alive, they'll be more cooperative, I'm sure. Especially Val. He looks to me like a man who likes to tell all."

"The way it seems to us," Benedict took over, "is that you set up this schedule, if you want to call it that. You supplied Cesare and Conti with the addresses, masterminded the operation as it were. Unless someone else was telling you what to do?"

"That's ridiculous!" She might dye her hair, but she had the temperament of a true redhead. "Why would I get mixed up in such a business? I'm a professional woman. I make a good living. You're out of your minds!"

"Let's see." I picked up my report on Margot Kline, baptized Margaret Kline, born in Providence, Rhode Island, mother, Mrs. Ethel Kline, now deceased, father unknown, date of birth, August 4, 1939. "When you were thirteen years old and living in Boston, you were taken into custody on complaint of your mother as an unmanageable child, you spent almost two years in the House of the Good Shepherd, then you were paroled into the custody of your mother, and at sixteen you were enrolled in hairdressing school. At eighteen, you ran away from home and there's a gap in the record of some four years when you were seeing the country and picking up some veneer, I suspect. You returned to Boston six years ago and worked for one of the big department stores in their beauty salon. You worked your way up to a managerial position before they fired you for suspected larceny, holding out on the cash receipts. They didn't prosecute because of lack of evidence. That's when you met Herman Agnew and talked him into opening La Femme." I smiled at her. "You see, we do a thorough job in short order when we have to. I began to put this little packet together last night and you'd be surprised at the number of people we've disturbed from their Sunday relaxation just to talk about you. We can recite the names of some old friends, too. Big names. Raymond Degman, the loan shark, for instance. Does that name ring any bells? And how about Sy Marrish—his specialty is the numbers—and Eddie Fairway—he's supposed to be very in with the syndicate."

She licked her lips. "I think I'd like to call Mr. Agnew. He was in Las Vegas, but he may be home now."

"Be our guest." I gestured toward the telephone. The lawyer Denbeaux looked uncomfortable and shuffled his feet.

She glared around at us, a caged animal look. The tiger

behind bars. I could have kicked myself from Division Two to the Common for not checking on her sooner. She reached for the phone and dialed a number with swift, talon-like fingers. No tiger, she. An eagle, bird of prey.

"Herman," she said, "this is Margot. I'm in trouble with the police."

Denbeaux cleared his throat, a warning.

She listened. "I know, I know," she said next, "but I couldn't help it. I need a lawyer, a good one." She gave Denbeaux a scornful glare. "That's the least you can do for me," she snapped at the telephone.

Another pause. "I'm damn sorry, but I don't care what you tell your wife. I'm a business associate, aren't I? You call this Frederick Franklin or whoever you said and get him over to Division Two pronto, you hear me!" She was about to say something else, but thought the better of it. Her lips closed tightly.

He had the final word. She didn't like what she was hearing, but she took it, then answered ungraciously, "I hear you, I hear you," and hung up.

"Now," said Margot Kline, "I've got nothing more to say. You can do your damnedest."

Herman Agnew lived on a virtual estate in Chestnut Hill. A three-story brick house with matching wings sat back on a large hedge-lined lot at the end of a long drive.

"I'd hate to shovel this driveway," I told Benedict.

"I wouldn't care to mow the lawn either."

"He's probably got one of those mowers you ride. A snow blower, too."

"Chances are he has help to take care of such mundane tasks."

"Chances are."

We stood politely at the door, having rapped with the ornate knocker, and waited. A motherly looking woman opened it, looked out inquiringly.

"Is Mr. Agnew in?"

"Who's calling, please?" She was well corseted and nicely but plainly dressed. Housekeeper or some such, I guessed.

"Tell him Mr. Severson and Mr. Benedict would like a word with him, please."

"Come in and wait. I'll tell him you're here."

We stood on a marble floor in an octagonal foyer. "Some house," I said.

"It used to be owned by some relative of the Lowells, I think." Benedict looked around. "Quite a step up from Roxbury."

The motherly looking woman appeared in a doorway to our oblique right. "Come in, please." We followed her into the room. It was a library, darkly paneled, its ceiling to floor shelves stacked with books.

Herman Agnew sat in a bay window at an antique desk. He was wearing a paisley robe and an ascot. He looked every inch the lord of the manor till you got to his face. That would spell tough guy as long as he lived.

"Good afternoon, gentlemen. This is Mrs. Agnew, Mr. Severson, Mr. Benedict." He stressed the mister. I stacked up the motherly looking woman against the likes of Margot Kline and got a clear picture.

Mrs. Agnew smiled and asked, "Would you care for coffee or a drink?"

I wanted her out of the room so I said, "Coffee would be fine."

She nodded and left us. We sat and looked at one another.

"I gather you're here about Margot Kline." Agnew closed a book he had been studying with a snap.

I put on my most congenial expression. "Yes, I guess you might call this a friendly, unofficial visit."

He shook his head sadly. "She called me. I sent my lawyer over. I don't believe in deserting a sinking ship. It's too bad."

"She's been working up to something like this for a long time. She has an interesting history, if you'd care to hear it. As you said, she's too greedy."

He placed his hands the way Granger was wont to do, fingertips together. It was a pious gesture. "I'll help her, of course. You realize that I have to. But, I presume, without avail. No doubt you have all the evidence you need."

"We hope so. Of course, it would help to locate Val Cesare and Julio Conti."

"I beg pardon? Oh, yes, now I remember. Two of the men who worked for her. Have they disappeared?"

"For the time being. They'll turn up."

"I'm sure they will." He fiddled with a letter opener. "Just what is it I can do for the police? Even though I must support Margot, old associations, you know, you realize that I am at your service."

"That's very law-abiding of you, I'm sure."

He gave me a quick look, over in an instant. "Sarcasm?" he asked.

I leaned forward, hands on my knees. "You are a very clever man, Mr. Agnew. We wanted to tell you that. When you're a cop, you have to learn at one time or another that there are some people you can't buck. You're one of them, sir."

He balanced the letter opener on one finger. It fell to the desk top.

"When I came to see you about La Femme, you were most cooperative. But of course we could plant a police officer in the shop. You merely had to say the word and it would be done. And I really admire your business acumen. You're such a first-rate businessman that you insisted the girl know the beauty shop routine. Twofold purpose there. You didn't want to waste an opportunity for a good worker for free and you wanted to tout us off Margot Kline. Margot, you said, would be suspicious if the girl weren't efficient. Subtle? My God, yes. The way you told me you couldn't trust her, for example. If you'd stood up for Margot's integrity, I might have looked into her past right then, just because I'm naturally suspicious of too-good-to-be-true people. I almost thought that about you, too, but once again you were too smart for me. By saying you didn't trust your mistress, you occupied my mind with thoughts of what a stinker you were. I call that sleight-of-hand. You're some magician."

We heard the tinkle of china on a tray so no one said anything. Mrs. Agnew carried it in, a big silver salver stacked with cups and saucers, pot, and plate of cookies, and set it down on the desk.

177

"Sugar and cream?" she asked.

"I'll do the honors, Thelma." Agnew stood up. "We're having a little business discussion. You don't mind . . ."

"Of course." Obediently, she went to the door. "Call me if you need anything."

"Maid's day off," Agnew explained. "Cream and sugar?"

"Black, please," Benedict requested.

"I'll do my own," I said.

When the cups had been distributed, we all sat down again, three mannerly fellows on a kaffeeklatsch.

"I'm afraid you're giving me too much credit." Agnew took up our conversation where we'd left off. "I'm just a hod carrier who made good."

"You'd like everyone to believe that. It must stand you in good stead on many an occasion. Gambling, for instance. I hear you've just returned from Las Vegas. The sharp boys think you're simple and just a little stupid, I imagine. But once would be enough for them. After that, they'd have you pegged and the word would get around. They're not sharp boys for nothing. Is that why you get kicks out of fostering a band of burglars? Because you've exhausted all the other fun and games?"

He looked bored. "It seems to me that the police have lost their touch. Too many books on psychology."

"Don't tell us you didn't know and approve of Margot Kline's little sideline." I put my cup and saucer down. "I'll bet I'd hardly put my foot out of your office when you had her on the telephone. They're onto us, you told her. They're going to put a female cop in your shop. Let's give them a run for their money. You sic her onto Val, you told Margot, and we'll give them something to think about. Besides, if worse comes to worse, Val and Dante are going to be the fall guys anyway. Val will play the weak sister and Dante can play the heavy and when they take the bait, whisk! You call some of your syndicate pals and ask them pretty please to get the patsys out of the way. That ought to keep the fuzz on their horses and off our backs. What did you do with Val and Dante, Agnew, just as a matter of curiosity? Did one of Margot's old mob friends kill them or did you just salt them away somewhere?"

Agnew leered at Benedict. "I'd suggest you have your associate see a doctor. He's having hallucinations. Or else, he's been taking LSD."

Benedict smiled pleasantly. "A year or two ago there was a game going around called the Doll game. Do you recall it, Mr. Agnew? It was a trivial game of pick-the-characteristics. A little homemade analysis with a pinch of acid."

Agnew blinked. "I don't follow you."

"I'll be more explicit. Say there's a Fidel Castro doll. You wind it up and it grows a beard and starts a revolution. Say there's an Elizabeth Taylor doll. You wind it up and it divorces Eddie Fisher and sails down the Nile with Richard Burton."

Agnew threw up his hands. "You're both crazy."

"Then there's a Herman Agnew doll. You wind it up and it makes money. It keeps on making money until it's up to its ears in money and then it begins to wind down. Is that all this Herman Agnew doll can do? Oh, no, it's a very complicated doll with many intricate parts needing constant lubrication. It's motivated by challenge, this Herman Agnew doll, that's what winds it up and oils it, but the challenges grow fewer and fewer until some of its parts are beginning to rust from lack of use."

"If you're trying to say I enjoy winning, you're right. Since when is that against the law?"

"Since the moment you picked the law as your worthy opponent. How did it happen, I wonder? A little tax manipulation, some hanky-panky with stocks and bonds? You will, I imagine, blame this scheme on Miss Kline but she's rather an unimaginative, run-of-the-mill lawbreaker, isn't she? An unprincipled satellite, circling the more common criminal constellations, drawn by gravity to the easy dollar. Such a cute little plan as this beauty shop setup isn't in her line at all. The person who dreamed that up had a sense of humor. And didn't care much for women, to boot."

He'd put his finger on a point. "Sure," I butted in. "What a joke on the vain female! Offer her instant beauty and steal her blind. You could sit back and laugh at us all, the police, women in general, men like Val and Dante who made their livings off such women, the whole shooting match."

"Power," said Benedict. "Omnipotent power."

"Don't give me that crap." Agnew scowled, his voice coarsened. "Everybody wants power. You cops are power-hungry. That's why you're cops. It starts from childhood, from the cradle. My old lady was the kind of mother who knew what power meant. One swipe of her hand and the world stood still."

"So you hated her," I goaded him.

"Hated her? Hell, no, I admired her. She knew the score backwards and forwards and she taught it to me. Trust nobody. Take anything you can get. And all the while, wear an innocent face. A simple philosophy that works. I ought to know. I live by it."

His voice had risen and we heard footsteps. He closed his mouth abruptly as Mrs. Agnew put her head inside the doorway. "Is something wrong, Herman? Did you want me?"

He changed his expression, his posture, his very personality before our eyes. He was Herman Agnew, reputable businessman, again. "No, my dear," he told her smoothly. "Just a spirited discussion. I'll call if we need anything."

She nodded diffidently and disappeared. When she had gone I asked, "Why didn't you tell her to shut up and mind her own business? I know you wanted to."

"Because I have taught myself control. Without control, man is a brainless animal. I am in control of Herman Agnew and thus I control others. People do as I say because they want to." He leaned back, pleased with himself. "You'll never convince my friends and associates that I masterminded these burglaries. To anyone who knows me, it would be inconceivable."

To myself I said, "Want to bet?" I gestured with my head toward the door. "How about Mrs. Agnew?"

His lip curled. "She wouldn't know what you're talking about. She's a very unworldly woman."

"Let's ask her, shall we?" I stood up. "We can tell her about Margot Kline and her friends, ask her if she's ever heard any telephone conversations, seen any communications or any confrontations. If you regard her so lightly, you can't have been careful all the time." I grinned mirthlessly. *"Cherchez la femme,* if you'll pardon the pun. As always."

"Her testimony would be worthless. She is my wife."

"The old bit about not testifying against a husband? Maybe she wouldn't, maybe she couldn't. But it would make interesting conversation, wouldn't it? For years to come, even."

Agnew took his time, poured himself a second cup of coffee. Another change had come over him and I knew that in some perverse way he was enjoying this. Because we were talking about him? Intense concentration on the many sides of Herman Agnew? "I'm afraid I underestimated you, Severson, and that's a high compliment because I seldom underestimate anyone. Just between us boys, and since the Supreme Court made confession as worthless as teats on a boar hog, I'll play along with you. I'll admit that I could find this sort of dangerous game amusing. Life can be pretty dull when you can buy anything you want. You need something to get excited about, like you did when you were a kid and you swiped a candy bar from the drugstore. Some of my contemporaries get their kicks by being do-gooders and I tried that, too; I've tried them all. But I'm too fond of a dollar to get any pleasure out of giving it away, especially to trash not worth a handout. So let's say Margot and I cooked up this little scheme one night between the sheets and it was fun while it lasted."

"I suppose you especially enjoyed the joke on Kay-Kay Mason."

He raised his eyebrows. "Who the hell is Kay-Kay Mason."

"She's a middle-aged alky who was trying to do her bit. She went into La Femme covered with diamonds to lure a heist and she must have come over like Mrs. Stool Pigeon because a trio of your boys—Margot's chums, were they?—I'd bet a month's salary that my rocky friend at the hospital can pick them out of a photo album—came out and beat the hell out of her. That's who Kay-Kay Mason is."

"That's the chance she took. I don't know anything about a Kay-Kay Mason. As for Margot's friends, I don't know any of Margot's friends, and furthermore, I don't care to know them."

"And I don't suppose you know who beaned Dorinda Prescott with a crystal ashtray either. Val and Julio were your moonlighters. Which one did it? I'd guess Val. He's the type to get panicky."

Agnew frowned, nodded. "That was stupid, really stupid. I told them in the beginning that violence was out. If they hadn't killed the woman, you'd never have gotten a sniff. As they explained it to me, they had no alternative. She knew him. She felt sorry for him, so she took a special interest in him. When she caught him in her inlaws' home, they had to get rid of her. No control. I told you, brainless animals. That's the trouble with business today. Too many nobodies going to college. Nobody with any intelligence left to be Indians. They're all going for chiefs."

I couldn't believe my ears. We might have been talking about carpenter's apprentices. I couldn't stop to wonder, though. Keep him talking. "They took a chance in breaking in the night before the Prescotts came home. Why wait till then?"

"A series of circumstances. This venture was a business, run like a business. We had a schedule to maintain. We'd already set up the jobs for Friday night and Saturday night. Then, the middle of that week, Mrs. Prescott got on the subject of her in-laws being away and due to return the first of the week. Val told Margot and Margot called me to see if we could fit it in. If we were going to do it at all, I said, it had to be Sunday. You've only got so much time to get everything done, you have to plan it. These things just don't fall into place like apples off a tree." He wiped his mouth with a napkin. "As it turned out, we should have passed it by."

"Greedy," I said. "There's the question of how they got into the safe. Did Dorinda Prescott give the combination or was it open? They didn't blow it. I presume you know. I can just imagine you holding Monday morning sales meetings with your weekend crew."

"It was open, can you beat that? Too easy. You learn to be suspicious when things are too easy."

"You can say that again. Well, I guess that just about does it for me. Anything you want to ask him, Benedict, before we pay a sick call on Kay-Kay?"

Benedict's tone was languid. "I've been sitting here trying to decide whether Agnew was born amoral or if he let his conscience die of starvation along the way. It doesn't bother you particularly that this girl was killed by your hirelings, does it, Agnew?"

Agnew pushed his upper lip over his lower lip. "You

184

don't listen well, Benedict. I said it before. I told them no violence."

"And having told them, this frees you of any responsibility?"

"You bleeding hearts are all alike. If I build a building and I hire a guy who's stupid enough to fall off the top of it, is that my fault?"

"I don't know," said Benedict softly. "Is it?"

"You know damn well it isn't. I sleep like a babe at night and I intend to go right on, free as a bird. You holier-than-thous can go frig yourselves. There's nothing you can do to get at me. I've read *Crime and Punishment* just like the rest of you intellectuals and damn dull reading it was. I'm not going to fill my head with a can of worms."

"I hope Mrs. Agnew shares your stoicism."

Muscles along Agnew's jawline moved. "What's Mrs. Agnew got to do with it? She lives in another world. A world I built for her, painted pink with singing angels."

"She won't be living there any more, will she? Especially after Margot Kline goes on trial."

There was a moment of silence.

We got to our feet. "Thanks for the coffee. Tell Mrs. Agnew good-by for us, will you?" I kept my face as pleasant as possible.

Agnew stood up. There was a cold smile on his face. He was getting kicks again, I could feel it. Margot Kline would take her lumps and like it, he was thinking. He'd make it worth her while to keep her pretty mouth closed very tight. Maybe he could. Maybe. She was greedy. But which came first, her money or her life?

"Of course," he said, "my pleasure."

He walked us to the door. I looked around in case the lady of the house was in earshot, but I didn't see her. The late afternoon September sun came in through the fan light, danced on the marble floor.

"Oh, Agnew, I almost forgot. I have a message for you from the commissioner," I said, my hand on the knob.

"Well, well. Is that so?"

"Yes. My captain and the commissioner had a long talk about you and he sent the word back. He said to tell you that he knows you do a lot of contract work for the city and state. He said that's really the way you make your big money. He said to tell you he doubted whether you'd be getting any of those fat contracts anymore. And maybe some government agency would be checking into some of the work you did do. You know, they've been awfully graft-conscious of late. Well, so long, Agnew. Don't take any wooden nickels."

14

On the way back from the hospital, where Kay-Kay was definitely sitting up and taking notice, I laid it on Benedict. "I want some advice, boy. Say there's this girl who's all screwed up in her thinking but she turns you on. Do you know what I mean?"

The sun was gone now and I couldn't see his expression too clearly. "I think so. Basically, I understand."

"Say she wants you to think the way she does, say she demands it or she won't have any part of you. What do you do?"

"What she asks is against your principles?"

"It sure is! Oh, it isn't illegal or anything like that. It's . . . well, I guess you could say it's man and woman business. Who runs the show, that kind of thing."

"And you're sure you're right?"

"For me, I'm right. For her, I don't know yet. I want

187

to find out if this is just a phase with either of us or if it's all the way through. Like a rotten spot in a lovely apple. She being the lovely apple, of course."

"Then I'd say you'd have to follow her rules until you make up your mind."

"I was afraid you'd say that."

"What did you want me to say?"

"What you did say, I guess."

Benedict laughed. After a second, I joined him.

"Any word on the baby?" I asked.

"Next Saturday. Will you come to the airport with us?"

"Sure, if you want me to. Funny, I feel better than I've felt in ages and only this morning I was sure this was the most fouled-up mess I'd ever seen."

"We didn't get Agnew."

"Except where it hurts. He'll be on our list from now on. Little rumors go out, to the tax people, the labor unions, the politicians. You shoot an arrow into the air, it falls to earth, you know not where!"

"I wonder," said Benedict thoughtfully, "what happened to Cesare and Conti?"

We found one of them, five days later. Val, floating face down near the Mystic River Bridge. As for Julio-Dante, we're still looking. Hopefully, he's hiding out in some self-made inferno. Or, maybe, he went the way of Val Cesare only the body went out to sea.

I telephoned Pat Drake and made my apologies. So far, she's condescended to have coffee with me once and a drink another time. But I'm making progress. She's fitted me into her coterie and we have a date for the final Red Sox game against Minnesota. She says if they win,

188

she might consider going with me to the World Series. If I sound sarcastic, it's because I could kick myself from here to Christmas. Where she's concerned, I'm damned if I do and damned if I don't. Now I know what they mean when they say, "I can't live with her and I can't live without her." If that's love, it's for the birds and I don't sing like any lark.

Still, all things considered, I went happily to the airport with Benedict and Barbara to greet the new arrival. Barbara was almost a nervous wreck; she kept asking Benedict to move her wheelchair, she couldn't see if the plane was coming.

Finally, it came in like a big bird and we went around to customs. I was beginning to get edgy, too. The feeling was contagious.

After forever, it seemed, one of the customs men came out and called Lawrence Benedict's name. He wheeled Barbara over to the customs man.

"I understand you've been expecting this young lady," said the customs man, and a tiny, young oriental woman, maybe five feet tall but she was a woman, not a child, I could tell from the shape of her, she had the tiniest waist I'd ever seen, walked out with a baby in her arms.

"This is Miss Lin," the customs official told us.

"And this," said Miss Lin in beautiful English, "is baby Kim." She bent down and put the infant in Barbara's lap.

"Oh!" said Barbara Benedict. "Oh." She bent her platinum head over the little dark-eyed baby. The baby looked up at her with wide wondering eyes. Benedict stood like a statue, his hands on the back of his wife's chair. He turned his head away from all of us and I thought he was crying. I couldn't just stand there, I had to do something.

"Miss Lin," I said, "you look like a girl who needs a cup of coffee. There's a coffee shop right over there. Will you join me?"

She glanced at her charge, at the Benedicts. "I'd be honored, sir," she said, and put a hand like a butterfly on my arm.